THE CURSE OF IRON EYES

Iron Eyes, the infamous bounty hunter, had taken on his greatest challenge. He rode into Waco to try to collect the bounty, not on one outlaw, but on an entire gang of ten. The Calhoon owlhoots were as mean as they came, but Iron Eyes did not easily frighten. Within minutes of arriving, he had killed them all — except for Harve Calhoon, their leader, who had somehow managed to slip away. Like a man possessed, Iron Eyes set out on Calhoon's trail — but the odds he faced were fearsome indeed.

RORY BLACK

THE CURSE OF IRON EYES

Complete and Unabridged

LINFORD
Leicester

First published in Great Britain in 2004 by
Robert Hale Limited
London

First Linford Edition
published 2005
by arrangement with
Robert Hale Limited
London

British Library CIP Data

Black, Rory
   The curse of Iron Eyes.—Large print ed.—
Linford western library
1. Western stories
2. Large type books
I. Title
823.9'14 [F]

ISBN 1–84395–613–6

Published by
F. A. Thorpe (Publishing)
Anstey, Leicestershire

Set by Words & Graphics Ltd.
Anstey, Leicestershire
Printed and bound in Great Britain by
T. J. International Ltd., Padstow, Cornwall

This book is printed on acid-free paper

Dedicated to my friend,
Colin Wall.

1

Blood ran down off the lush red velvet-covered walls, but was hardly noticeable until it reached the highly polished floorboards. Then it blended into the rest of the horrific pool of quickly drying crimson gore spread evenly between the six dead bodies which were scattered all around the bounty hunter.

The tall thin emaciated figure moved slowly through the gunsmoke like a phantom seeing a new place to haunt. His eyes darted all around him as he moved determinedly on. There was no time to waste thinking about what he had just done. He had to concentrate on what had yet to be achieved.

For it was far from over.

He had only been in this place for a mere three minutes according to the wall clock that continued to tick on the far wall. But in those three short minutes the bounty hunter had already killed all who had tried to stop his progress towards his ultimate goal.

Killing the leaders of the Calhoon gang.

The photographic likenesses of each of them were on the crumpled Wanted posters pushed down into the deep pockets of the long trail coat. Frank and Harve Calhoon were worth $6,000 between them and their cousin Dale Smith another $2,000. Rob John Floyd was reputed to be the actual brains of the gang and yet his value was only $1,000.

None of this mattered to the bounty hunter though. He had chosen to claim the bounty on all their heads and that was what he intended to do.

Smoke traced from the pair of Navy Colts as the long thin legs of their owner stepped over one body after another on his way towards the high staircase.

He knew that the four of them were

up there somewhere, hiding in any of the dozen or more rooms that served to make this place the most profitable building of its kind anywhere west of Dodge.

The walls still resounded to the echoes of the bullets that had blasted through the cigar-smoke-filled rooms as the awesome figure strode on.

There was no escape.

He had their scent in his nostrils and was closing in on them for the ultimate kill. His calculating mind had already worked out that he had earned nearly a $1,000 by destroying the outlaws lying at his feet.

But the biggest prize of all was still to be had. The Calhoons were up there behind the solid oak doors.

His long skeletal fingers quickly reloaded the pair of guns before his mule-ear boots stepped on to the luxurious carpet at the foot of the flight of stairs.

Without pausing for even a single moment, Iron Eyes continued up towards the well-illuminated landing. With each step, the sound of his razor-sharp spurs rang out around the wooden building.

Their ominous jangling was like the warning bells of death tolling for those who knew that the Grim Reaper was headed straight for them.

Most of the females who worked in this place had fled in terror as the lead had started to fly. But Iron Eyes knew that there had to be more of them upstairs and that the men he sought would more than likely try to use them as human shields to avoid the lethal lead of his Navy Colts.

Iron Eyes would not be so easily dissuaded from using his lethal guns though.

He would not deliberately kill any female but if they got in his way, he would shoot through them. For he wanted the bounty money on the heads of his prey.

For that was what the Calhoons were to the bounty hunter.

They were his prey and they were wanted.

Dead or Alive. To Iron Eyes, that meant dead. He had no time for prisoners.

When he reached the landing, he paused. Iron Eyes lowered his head and stared through the long black strands of hair that hung before his eyes. He knew that behind one or more of these closed doors, men waited for him with their guns cocked and ready.

Just like his own Navy Colts were.

He listened and waited.

It seemed that the only sound he could hear was his own heart beating hard inside his thin chest. The stench of gunsmoke had risen to where he stood. It reminded him of the job that was still unfinished.

Iron Eyes did not move a muscle. Only his eyes moved as he studied the layout before him. There were an equal number of doors on either side of the corridor which faced the barrels of his still-smoking guns. It was not the way he liked to hunt, but there had been far worse places that he had found himself drawn into when he was closing in on the faces that appeared on the crumpled Wanted posters in his deep jacket pockets.

He inhaled deeply.

A noise along the corridor caught his attention. It was the muffled sobbing of a female. He began to stride silently like a panther along the carpeted floor towards the sound.

This was going to be bloody. He knew that. The men who had tried to stop him below had only been the hired help of those who were up here with the soiled doves.

The men he was after were far better with their weaponry and yet he was unafraid.

For fear to Iron Eyes was something that he had never experienced in his entire life. Only men with something to live for fear dying. And Iron Eyes had never had anything to live for.

He simply existed.

Further and further he ventured along the corridor towards the room where his keen hearing told him that a woman had a hand across her mouth. Glass oil-lamps decorated the length of the long corridor. They were suspended on brass hoops that were screwed to the walls.

Then it happened.

Three of the doors swung open.

Swiftly, Iron Eyes raised both his pistols to shoulder-height.

There were two to his left and one to his right. One behind him, one level with him and the third, slightly ahead of him. Each of the outlaws held their partially clothed female hostages tightly with their left arms whilst their right hands gripped their primed guns. The barrels of their pistols came jutting out of the dark interiors of the rooms allowing the lamplight to dance off them.

Faster than seemed possible, Iron Eyes turned with his guns at arm's length. In the time it takes for a heart to beat just once, the bounty hunter had spotted that all three outlaws had done exactly as he had expected.

Each of the vermin was using the near-naked females as human shields.

The cold steel-coloured eyes of the bounty hunter narrowed as they sought their targets. He only required a glimpse of the wanted men, to be able to hit his targets with his deadly bullets.

All three outlaw guns exploded into action. It was like a fireworks display on the Fourth of July. The lethal red-hot tapers sped at Iron Eyes from three different directions. Bullets rained in at him.

The acrid stench of the choking gunsmoke soon filled the length of the corridor.

As the wall around him was torn into shreds by the deadly lead, Iron Eyes dropped on to one knee and felt the plaster showering over his head and broad shoulders.

The oil-lamps that were attached to the corridor walls began to explode as stray bullets shattered their glass globes. With each shot that was fired, it was getting darker. Iron Eyes had very little target to aim at and yet his deadly accuracy once again did not fail him.

He sent a bullet over the shoulder of one of the females and saw the head of Frank Calhoon virtually explode. The girl dropped to her knees as gore ran down her back. Her screams were almost as deafening as the sound of the pistols that were being fired in the narrow confines of the corridor.

Without even a second's hesitation, the bounty hunter threw himself across the floor. He landed on his back and fired both his Navy Colts above his head at the furthest open doorway. This time his shot went beneath the near-naked red-haired girl and smashed into the startled outlaw's ribs.

The wounded outlaw released his grip on her and staggered into the frame of the door. Iron Eyes blasted two more bullets into the centre of his already helpless target.

He did not wait to watch Rob John Floyd falling. He knew that the outlaw was dead.

Iron Eyes had seen the red-haired girl running away from the carnage before he leapt back to his feet.

The last of the wanted men could see that having a human shield was no protection against such a marksman. He pushed the female toward Iron Eyes. The bounty hunter was knocked off balance and felt the Colt in his left hand fire. The bullet went straight up and hit one of the few remaining oil-lamps. The glass bowl exploded.

Liquid fire cascaded over the girl as they both fell backwards and hit the floor.

Iron Eyes saw her hair ignite only inches in front of his face as his back hit the wall.

She screamed in agony. It was the most chilling sound that he had ever heard.

The bounty hunter reached out and pulled her blazing head into his jacket.

He smothered the flames with his own shirt and leather coat.

Iron Eyes could feel his own skin burning, but did not acknowledge the pain. He watched the outlaw slam the door opposite them.

Iron Eyes released the screaming girl. Her hair was still smouldering. It was a stench that sickened even him. He rose to his feet and heard the sound of the bolt being pushed into place behind its solid oak door.

He knew that he could waste a lot of expensive bullets trying to get into that room and still not achieve his goal.

Iron Eyes ignored the wailing hysteria of his terrified audience and marched down the corridor until he found a window.

He turned its latch and then pushed the window away from him, staring out into the darkness. A balcony went all the way around the side and front of the building.

Iron Eyes tore the lace drapes from the window and then poked his long left leg out and followed it. He was still gripping on to his Navy Colts. Then saw a window roughly fifteen feet away from him opening.

That was the window to the room that the outlaw had locked himself into, he thought.

He began to walk silently towards the open window.

As the outlaw clambered out on to the balcony with his gun in one hand and his clothes in the other, he did not even think to look behind him. His eyes were fixed on the bolted door which he expected the bounty hunter to try and shoot his way through at any moment.

It came as quite a shock to the outlaw when he heard the eerie voice behind him.

'Going someplace, Dale Smith?' Iron Eyes breath chilled the man's naked spine.

Smith turned and saw the gruesome sight before him. He had heard tales of the bounty hunter who, it was claimed, was more dead than alive.

As his eyes adjusted to the darkness, Smith knew that there was no description which could come close to describing the way this man looked. The long, limp, black hair over the scarred features did not make this creature look any less horrific.

'Are you Iron Eyes?'

'Yep.'

'I ain't got no beef with you.'

'This ain't personal, Smith.' Iron Eyes said coldly. 'You're wanted dead or alive and as far as I'm concerned, that means dead.'

'So you've made yourself judge and jury, huh?'

'Yep.'

Smith's gun barrel began to move.

Both Navy Colts fired. Smith went spinning on his heels. His clothes flew over the balcony and floated down into the street as he bounced off the balcony rail. Smith raised his gun and squeezed its trigger. His bullet seemed to pass through the bounty hunter as Iron Eyes fired both his weapons again.

13

Smith was thrown backwards. His body hit the wooden boards hard.

Iron Eyes pushed one of his Navy Colts into his belt and then ran his fingers across his stinging side. He stared at the blood on the tips of his fingers and sighed.

'Close, but no cigar, Smith. You've obviously bin used to shooting much fatter men.'

2

It was a vision that would have frozen the blood in the veins of most men. Marshal Tad Barker stared hard at the foreboding figure before him trying to convince himself that it was indeed human and not something from dark depths of his nightmares.

As the flickering street-lanterns tried to fend off the blackness of night, sweat traced down the side of the seasoned law officer's face. He held on tightly to the cocked scattergun in his weathered hands and tried to swallow. Barker was thankful that he had not been foolhardy enough to satisfy his curiosity on his own.

For the strange figure before him was not the sort of man any sane person would wish to meet alone.

He had mustered every single deputy within the streets of Waco when he had heard the sound of gunfire emanating from the Red Garter House, before daring to venture towards it. The sight of Iron Eyes standing on the raised porch amid the array of bodies chilled even his cold heart.

The tails of the trail coat flapped in the evening breeze in tune to the beat of his long, matted black hair.

The marshal raised the primed scattergun across his chest and strode purposefully towards the bounty hunter with his six deputies spread evenly to either side of him.

In his long eventful life, Barker had faced hostile Indians and the cannon of a bitter enemy during the war, but he had never faced anyone who looked anything like Iron Eyes before.

For the first time in his life, he felt totally afraid. Iron Eyes still held one of his Navy Colts in his bony left hand as he bent over his victims and added up the financial tally he had just earned.

It was like witnessing a vulture in human form checking the carcasses it was about to feed upon.

The bounty hunter squinted through the lantern light at the seven lawmen who approached him and then stood upright. He lowered his pistol and stepped to the edge of the boardwalk as Barker reached it.

'Marshal.' The word came through Iron Eyes' small sharp teeth.

'You seem to have bin on a killing spree, stranger,' the marshal said carefully. 'I hope you got yourself a darn good reason.'

'I'm a bounty hunter. I claim the bounty on these varmints' heads,' Iron Eyes said. He reached into his deep pocket and pulled out the crumpled Wanted posters.

Barker signalled to one of his deputies. There was no way that the marshal was about to release his grip on his weapon to accept anything from the terrifying figure, just in case it was a trap and he started killing again. A cautious deputy stepped forward and took the posters from the thin skeletal hand and unfolded them.

'What they say, Clem?' Barker asked as his index finger remained on the twin triggers of the scattergun and his eyes remained glued to the bounty hunter.

The deputy named Clem looked up from the posters.

'Looks like we have us the remains of the Calhoon boys here, Tad.'

Barker raised an eyebrow and took his eyes briefly away from the tall figure of Iron Eyes and glanced at the bloody pile of corpses stacked before him. It was impossible to identify any of the bodies clearly in the shadows that bathed the front of the whorehouse.

'If this is the Calhoon gang, it looks like you've made yourself a lotta money this night, stranger,' the marshal said, spitting at the ground beside him before starting to chew the tobacco plug in his mouth once more.

Suddenly, Iron Eyes looked troubled.

'The name's Iron Eyes, Marshal,' he said coldly. He turned back towards the bodies again. He stuffed the pistol into his belt beside the other and then paced around the blood-soaked corpses again.

'What's wrong, Iron Eyes?' Barker asked. His hooded eyes watched the bounty hunter bending over and lifting each of the outlaws' heads off the boardwalk in turn.

'How many posters have you got there, boy?' Iron Eyes asked the deputy called Clem as he studied his handiwork.

Clem cleared his throat and hastily counted the crumpled sheets of paper in his hands.

'Ten, Mr Iron Eyes. Why?'

'Damn!' Iron Eyes kicked the lifeless head of Rob John Floyd in anger. 'I missed one of the bastards.'

Marshal Barker looked at the equally confused faces of his deputies on either side of him, then returned his gaze to the strange, tall figure above him.

'What you mean, Iron Eyes?'

'There are only nine here. That means that one of the Calhoon boys got

19

away by the looks of it.' Iron Eyes snatched the posters from the deputy's hand and methodically compared each dead outlaw face with the crude images on the paper. 'Harve Calhoon!'

'What about him?' Barker piped up before spitting out another dark lump of spittle.

'He's the one that's missing.' Iron Eyes rammed the posters back into the hands of the nervous Clem and drew both his Navy Colts again. He cocked their hammers, then turned and marched back into the large building.

Barker trailed the bounty hunter into the gunsmoke filled saloon. There was blood and chunks of flesh covering everything. The aroma of death hung on the air. The marshal trailed the long-legged man up the flight of stairs to the landing. He maintained a respectable distance between himself and the snorting Iron Eyes.

Marshal Barker paused at the top of the stairs and watched the bounty hunter kicking open every door. The screams of the terrified women inside the rooms echoed all around the building while Iron Eyes continued his frenzied search.

When he could not find any sign that the outlaw had ever been in this place with his brother and rest of his gang, the tall brooding man stopped and rested his back against the wall which was still wet from the blood of his victims.

Barker walked slowly toward Iron Eyes and nodded at each of the females huddled in the rooms as he passed them. The keen eyes of the lawman then spied the sobbing girl with the smouldering hair crumpled in a doorway.

He paused and knelt down beside her. She was burned down one side of her face and across her shoulder. The injuries were already festering in the humid air.

'Katie?' Barker whispered.

She looked up into his fatherly eyes

and then glanced across at the silent Iron Eyes who was deep in thought at the end of the corridor.

'I ought to get you over to Doc Harper, Katie,' the marshal said lowering his scattergun on to the floor and removing his jacket and placing it carefully around her shoulders.

She winced as the lawman lifted her to her feet.

'Who is that?' Katie asked quietly.

'No need to be afraid of him. He's just a bounty hunter.'

'I'm not afraid of him, Marshal,' she said as Barker scooped his scattergun up off the bloodstained carpet. 'He smothered the flames when the oil-lamp spewed burning oil all over me.'

Barker glanced at Iron Eyes.

'He did?'

'He must have been burned himself doing it,' Katie added. 'He risked his life to help me in the middle of the gunfight, Marshal Barker.'

Iron Eyes pushed himself away from the wall and marched past the two talking figures. They watched as he ran down the flight of stairs and out into the street.

By the time Barker had led the injured girl out into the dimly illuminated street, the bounty hunter was fifty yards away checking the horses that were tied to the hitching rails.

'Take Katie over to Doc Harper, Clem,' Barker told the deputy as he waved his hand at the rest of his men. 'Drag them bodies over to my office, boys. I want to match them to them Wanted posters before paying out any bounty.'

Iron Eyes ran his hand along the neck of the last of the horses and then squared up to the lawman as he walked up to him. 'I figure that Harve Calhoon was never here with the rest of his gang, Marshal,' Iron Eyes said, pushing the pistols back into his belt. 'But why not?'

Barker stared at the pearl-handled gun-grips that poked out from the almost flat stomach of the bounty hunter. He then noticed the burned shirt and the visible scars across the chest of Iron Eyes. He found it hard to comprehend that this strange creature would have helped Katie in the middle of a blazing gun battle. But he had.

'What the hell are you, Iron Eyes?'

Iron Eyes ran his long bony fingers through his limp hair and pushed it off his face. The sight was enough to make the marshal's throat go dry. It was a face that had endured many battles and each of them was carved into his scarred features. If Iron Eyes had ever truly resembled other men, it must have been a very long time ago, Barker thought.

'I'm just a bounty hunter. Why?'

'I've met a lotta bounty hunters. They weren't nothing like you,' Barker croaked.

Iron Eyes shrugged and looked at the bodies being carried by the deputies. He then glanced back at Barker.

'Whatever the tally for them critters

comes to, give it to the girl you called Katie.'

Before the marshal could respond, the long legged man had walked away into the darkness.

3

The trail led due south. Iron Eyes was back-tracking the Calhoon gang's route to Waco, but it was not an easy task. A sand storm had been threatening for hours and at last started to blow. The dusty surface layer of the dry sand was blowing hard and fast across the arid prairie as the bounty hunter forced his weary pony on.

The mount was spent and needed food and water but Iron Eyes cared little for horses. He just kept ramming his razor-sharp spurs into its already bloody flesh. He wanted to catch up with the outlaw who had somehow slipped away from the rest of the now dead gang.

Nothing else mattered.

Only pride in finishing a job that he had started.

Most of the tracks had been blown

away, but not all. There were still enough left for the experienced hunter to steer his pony on toward his goal.

The bounty hunter knew that somewhere along the fifty-mile trail that had led him after the ruthless outlaws, he must have somehow missed wherever it was that Harve Calhoon had left the main group.

It was the first time that anyone had managed to outwit the skilled hunter. But then, the ride to Waco had been the first time that Iron Eyes had trailed ten wanted men at once. He had taken on groups of four or five gunfighters before and dispatched them easily, but the Calhoon gang had been the biggest and most tricky prize that he had ever tried to catch and kill.

As he rode feverishly on, a thought kept haunting the deadly Iron Eyes; why had Harve Calhoon cut away from the main group of outlaws at all?

And where had the varmint gone?

Apart from Waco, there was little else to attract a ruthless bank robber.

Or was there? Perhaps Calhoon knew something about this barren territory that he had yet to learn.

The trail was mercilessly hot the further south that Iron Eyes rode. Yet nothing could stop him now. He was angry and wanted the last of the once notorious Calhoon gang dead.

There was no other way.

Harve Calhoon had disappeared, but Iron Eyes knew that there was nowhere for the outlaw to hide once he located the exact spot where he had cut away from his nine fellow-outlaws.

The bounty hunter would seek him out wherever Calhoon tried to hide.

The trail began to rise slowly up a sandy dune. The exhausted pony continued being spurred hard by its master. Iron Eyes knew that he had to continue following what remained of the trail if he were ever to discover where Calhoon had managed to do the seemingly impossible, and get away from the most infamous hunter of men in the West.

It never once crossed his mind that even if he had seen the tell-tale signs in the sand which would have alerted him that one of the gang had split away from the others, he could not have followed both trails. He would have still tracked the larger group on to Waco.

Iron Eyes whipped his pony viciously with the ends of his long reins and managed to make the hapless creature climb to the crest of the soft, sandy dune.

The sight that met the steel-grey-coloured eyes caused Iron Eyes to haul his reins up to his chest. He sat silently astride the lathered-up mount and watched the approaching Apache warriors. They had obviously spotted the dust which rose thirty feet into the air off the hoofs of his pony, long before he had been aware of them.

There were eight of them and they were all painted for battle.

Iron Eyes gritted his teeth and stood in his stirrups to give him a better view of the land that surrounded him. It was hotter than Hell itself on the crest of the sandy rise but the grim-faced rider knew that it could and probably would get even hotter in only a few minutes if he did not act swiftly.

Whatever had riled up the Indians, it must have been bad, he concluded. They rode their painted ponies straight at him and screamed their haunting war cries.

He could see the sun glinting off their rifles and war lances as the Apache hunting party galloped closer and closer. Yet Iron Eyes held his mount in check.

There was still not one ounce of fear in any part of him.

For however much paint the Apache warriors had covering their faces and bodies, they were still only men. And there had never been a man born that frightened Iron Eyes.

His long thin arm reached behind him and slid out his seldom-used Winchester from the long scabbard beneath his saddle. He tried to crank its mechanism but it was stiff and unyielding.

Iron Eyes knew that it was quite easy to kill riders, any riders with the aid of a fourteen-shot repeating rifle, but not this one. He snarled and rammed the barrel of the Winchester back into the scabbard. He knew that it would take at least an hour to clean and oil the carbine before it was possible to use it on the charging Indians.

At the speed that they were approaching, he had less than two minutes. He ran the fingers of both hands through his long limp hair and glared at them. He was going to have to do this the hard way.

Up close with his Navy Colts and long Bowie knife, it was going to be yet another blood-bath. But this time, it was not one of his own making. He had no wish to kill anyone who did not have a price on his head. Yet Iron Eyes knew that this bunch of furious Indians did not look as though they wanted to do anything except kill him.

There was another choice available to the bounty hunter and yet it was one that he refused even to acknowledge. It meant turning his already exhausted mount and riding away.

For Iron Eyes, there was no retreat.

There never had been and there never would be.

He spun his mount full circle and studied the terrain which seemed little different whatever direction he looked in. There was little or no cover to be had anywhere. That meant that he had to remain right where he was, and fight.

When you fought Apaches you had to kill them or they would most certainly kill you. Like Iron Eyes, they never took prisoners.

His mount was nervous as it sensed the approaching riders bearing down on them. It gnashed at its bit and tried to turn away from the yelling warriors who were thundering ever closer.

Suddenly, over his shoulder, something caught his attention far behind him. Iron Eyes swung his pony around again and stared hard off into the distance along the trail that he had just ridden along.

He could see the dust rising into the dry air from the hoofs of a rider who was following him.

A rider who was at least an hour or so behind him.

'Somebody's following us, horse!' the bounty hunter growled curiously. 'But who? Don't that idiot know that only death rides on my trail?'

The sound of rifle shots came from the approaching Apaches behind him. Iron Eyes snarled and spun his pony around once more, then he felt the sudden impact beneath his saddle. The pony shuddered. Blood spurted out from two wounds in its chest.

Then the mount gave out a deafening whine.

More shots burned through the dry hot air.

Iron Eyes glanced up and saw the plumes of gun smoke coming from a few of the leading Apaches' rifles. A bullet passed through his hair and nicked the lobe of his left ear.

Then more shots tore into the animal as its startled master fought with the reins in a vain attempt to keep the creature on its feet.

His mount staggered and then toppled forward on to its head and neck.

Iron Eyes hit the ground hard.

4

The man who had long been thought of as a living ghost had hit the ground hard when his injured pony had collapsed beneath him. Iron Eyes hurt real bad, but he knew that there was no time left to dwell upon anything except the thundering Apache mounts behind him. He rolled over in the burning-hot sand and saw that the eight chanting warriors were closing in with every heartbeat but the pathetic noise of his pony drew his attention from their rifle fire. The bounty hunter looked back at the injured pony beside him and pulled both guns from his belt. Without a second thought, he pushed one of the weapons against the temple of the shaking animal and fired.

The pony slumped into the soft sand. Dragging himself up on to one knee,

Iron Eyes knew that at least the animal's suffering was over. His own fate was less predictable.

Arrows landed several yards ahead of him as yet more rifle bullets tore through the hot air. He felt them passing all around him. Then he raised his Navy Colts.

The eight Apaches had made good time.

They were now bearing down on him at incredible speed. He cocked the hammers of both pistols and trained them on his attackers.

Then Iron Eyes waited.

He had nerves of steel.

There was not one bead of sweat on him as his cold eyes focused down the barrels of his primed handguns. He knew that to fire too soon was to waste valuable ammunition. He had to wait until they were in the range of his deadly weaponry as their rifle bullets rained in at him.

It took courage but he had plenty of that.

He began to wonder; why were they so all-fired up?

The question kept hammering into his mind.

Yet if there were people whom he liked to kill almost as much as wanted outlaws, it was Apaches.

The Indians were looking for a fight and he was going to grant their dying wish. They had started the trouble, but Iron Eyes was determined that it would be he who finished it.

Their bullets ripped through the loose tails of his long trail coat, but Iron Eyes remained as still as a statue. Their arrows got closer and closer to where he knelt, but he did not blink.

When he could see the whites of their eyes, he knew it was time. They were within the range of his trusty matched Navy Colts.

With an expertise and speed that few men could equal, Iron Eyes squeezed his triggers with his index fingers and haul the hammers back with his thumbs.

Shot after shot came spewing from the barrels of his lethal Navy Colts at the native horsemen who bore down on him. Bullets and arrows rained at Iron Eyes but still he did not flinch.

One by one the Apache braves were torn from the backs of their painted ponies. One by one they felt the deadly lead of Iron Eyes's accuracy.

The bounty hunter quickly rose to his feet when he felt both his guns were empty. Knowing that there was no time to reload them, Iron Eyes dropped them on to the sand at his feet. He hauled the long Bowie knife from his right boot and ran at the last two screaming riders.

Before the first warrior could train his long rifle at Iron Eyes, it was hauled from his grasp. The bounty hunter leapt up on to the back of the Indian's pony. It reared up, sending both men crashing into the sand. Iron Eyes felt the fist of the winded brave catch him on his jaw, but it did not stop him. The knife was thrust into the belly of the Indian.

It claimed its victim instantly.

Iron Eyes gritted his teeth and then grabbed at the mane of the startled pony and stopped it from galloping after all the other horses. It took every ounce of his strength but he held the pony in check as his keen eyes watched the last of the warriors turning his own mount to face him.

They were twenty yards apart and Iron Eyes was using the skittish animal as a shield.

For a brief moment both men looked straight into each other's souls. They paused and each sought a weakness in his enemy.

The Apache screamed a spine-chilling war cry and kicked his mount into action once more. With every stride, the warrior fired his Winchester at the pony and the man who stood behind it. Bullets tore into the painted horse and it reared up. It then collapsed, leaving the bounty hunter exposed.

He watched the Indian galloping straight at him.

As the pony reached him, Iron Eyes side-stepped the unshod hoofs and threw himself up and over the back of the painted pony.

Iron Eyes grappled with the ferocity of a mountain lion on the back of the pony. Then he felt the blanket slip off the back of the startled animal. The two men hit the ground at exactly the same time.

The rifle went hurtling out of the warrior's hand as the Apache grabbed at the right wrist of Iron Eyes. The long blade of the Bowie knife glinted in the blazing sunlight. Both men wrestled across the sand, neither of them willing to release his grip on the other.

A naked knee rammed into the belly of the bounty hunter. Iron Eyes felt his ribs buckle before he fell off the snarling Indian and rolled on to his back.

The brave still held on firmly to the wrist of Iron Eyes and tried to kick his enemy senseless. Yet the moccasin was no match for the hefty mule-ear boot. Iron Eyes drew up both his knees and kicked out as hard as he was able.

The Apache went flying backwards, yet before Iron Eyes could get up off the ground, the Indian had recovered and thrown himself back on top of him.

Iron Eyes lunged out but felt the strong fingers grab his wrist once again. A punch smashed into the face of the winded hunter of men before he could block it. Somehow Iron Eyes managed to shake his knife-hand free and lashed out with its deadly blade. He saw the Indian wince as its razorsharp edge glanced across the naked chest of the painted warrior.

Iron Eyes pushed his opponent away for a brief moment and then saw the bleeding Indian dragging his own knife from its leather sheath and stagger back to his feet. They were only a matter of yards away from one another, staring into each other's eyes.

Both knew as they gripped their

knives in their bloodstained hands that within a few moments, one of them was going to die. But it was a good day to fight and a good day to die.

They charged towards one another.

5

The knives flashed in the sunlight. Each man cut and thrust with nothing on his mind except the ultimate destruction of his equally determined opponent.

In very different ways, the two blood-drenched men were warriors. Each had learned to kill so long ago that neither knew any other way to exist.

It was part of what they were. They killed. Without emotion or regret, they simply killed.

Blood trailed across the white sand around the two men. Iron Eyes knew that he had been caught more than a dozen times by the lethal Apache blade yet he continued fighting. His own Bowie knife had slashed the painted flesh of the smaller, more agile Indian as many times.

The two bleeding men circled one another leaving trails of crimson droplets on the hot sand. There was nothing now in their fevered minds except death.

Each was equally confident in his own ability to destroy the other.

Iron Eyes knew that he had an advantage, being far taller than the warrior before him, but this was no protection against the darting knife that ripped at his already shredded shirt.

The Apache slashed out with the knife again. Its honed tip sliced through the bounty hunter's sleeve. Iron Eyes could feel even more blood trailing down his arm.

There was only one way to have a chance of killing this foe, and it required that he used his superior height. Fighting up close meant giving the smaller man a target he could not miss and the multitude of bleeding wounds on the torso of Iron Eyes were testament to the warrior's skill.

The Apache leapt once again toward

his tall, ghostlike target and used his knife again.

Iron Eyes kicked out at the Apache and forced him backward once again. He glanced down at his right hand and saw the bloody gash across the back of it.

Keeping his keen eyes on the crouching figure before him, the bounty hunter switched his knife into his left hand, then slipped out of his long trail coat and dropped it on to the blood-soaked sand.

There was nothing in the face opposite him to give Iron Eyes any hint of what the skilled warrior would do next. But he knew that whatever it was, it would hurt. Just as every one of the countless other bleeding wounds also hurt. It felt as if half the surface of his skin had been attacked by crazed hornets.

Iron Eyes was angry with himself for not being able to finish this straight-away. He had missed the opportunity to kill the Indian swiftly. Now he was paying with blood for that mistake.

Crimson gore trailed from the numerous gashes all over the tall man as he stared at the wounds of his deadly foe. He too was covered in the vicious scars of their encounter. So far, they seemed to have inflicted an equal number of injuries on each other, neither man having been able to administer one last lethal strike.

Iron Eyes took a step backward and then moved his feet behind his discarded coat.

He had somehow to use his greater height and reach if he were to kill this man. If he did not, he knew that it would be the Apache who would triumph.

The crouching Indian leaned forward and charged for the umpteenth time. The sun flashed across the knife blade which was held high above the warrior's head.

Iron Eyes knew he had to act swiftly.

He scooped the toe-point of his right boot under the coat and kicked it up into the air between them. The coat was heavy with the bullets which filled its deep pockets, but it still rose just high enough to hit the charging warrior in his face and stop his advance.

The Indian staggered for a few seconds, but it was more than enough time for the bounty hunter to act.

He strode across the sand and kicked at the Apache. He caught the near-naked brave low and watched the man's head drop. The second kick caught the warrior in his face.

Before the stunned Apache hit the sand, Iron Eyes had buried the full length of his Bowie knifeblade into him.

Iron Eyes twisted the deadly dagger and heard the shocked gasp come from his victim's mouth. He could feel the air leaving the burst lung over his hand as they both hit the ground.

He withdrew the blood-covered blade and then stabbed his opponent again and again. There was a madness in the frenzied attack but the bounty hunter wanted to ensure that he had finally finished off this opponent.

Iron Eyes continued ramming the knife into the helpless warrior's chest long after the man was dead.

For the first time in his entire life, Iron Eyes had come within a whisker of being defeated in combat. It was a situation that he found hard to understand.

When the pupils of his cold grey eyes focused at last on the dead body beneath him, he rose quickly to his feet and turned away. He staggered back to his coat and lifted it off the hot sun-baked sand. Then paused.

He stared all around him at the lifeless bodies which were strewn across the white sand.

Iron Eyes slid the knife back into the neck of his right boot and then hauled the heavy trail coat on to his bleeding body. He staggered around, looked down at his dead pony lying where it had fallen only a few minutes earlier.

Then he concentrated on the closest Indian pony.

It took every ounce of his remaining strength to remove the coiled rope off his saddle and face the scattered Indian mounts. He knew that he had to try and capture one of the fallen warriors' ponies if he were to carry on in pursuit after the elusive Harve Calhoon and escape this place.

Slowly he began to spin the rope above his head.

He then recalled the rider who had been following him.

Even though he knew that it might take the rider an hour to reach this spot, there was no time to waste. He had to capture one of the nervous mounts and ride out of here before that rider caught up with him.

For the first time in his brutal existence, Iron Eyes did not want to fight. He was exhausted and needed time to heal. There had been enough blood spilled this day and a lot of it was his own.

The rope was spinning above his head faster and faster as he glared at his chosen target. He unleashed the rope and watched its twirling loop encircle the neck of the closest of the painted ponies. He pulled on the rope and watched its loop tighten around the horse's neck.

Slowly he began to draw the creature towards him.

6

It was known as Devil's Pass. It had earned the name long before any of the men who rode across its blazing-hot sand between the high, narrow canyon walls were born. Even the once numerous Apache knew better than to spend too long in the place which, it was said, had been created by the Devil himself to capture lost souls.

For this was a place where nothing lived for long. It had a thousand ways to kill and it had used them all on the unwary.

Situated less than a score of miles away from the 7th Cavalry's most westerly outpost, Fort Dixon, Devil's Pass was the only direct route to Waco from the north. Yet even so, few ventured into its deadly canyons which stretched for scores of lifeless miles. There were safer routes that encircled the entire region and had dozens of smaller trails leading to various other towns situated on the edge of the territory.

But for all its hidden dangers, Devil's Pass still provided a short cut to those who dared to enter its unforgiving canyons. There was always someone either ignorant or foolhardy enough to risk his life by venturing into it.

The nervous platoon seldom rode into Devil's Pass, because of its deadly reputation, but on this day, it had done so. For some reason that only Captain Hugh Wallis was privy to, they had been ordered to ride straight through its winding hot canyons.

Each man in the cavalry wondered why. What could be so important? Only Wallis knew the answer and he was saying nothing.

His orders had been sealed when they had left Fort Dixon. He had been instructed not to open them until he had led his men to the mouth of the great canyon.

Whatever were the details contained in the orders, Wallis had done exactly as they commanded. He had then folded up the two pages and placed them in his breast pocket.

He did not reveal anything to the men in his command. But each of them knew that it had to be very important for him to be leading them into this place. Something was brewing and they could taste it on the dry sand that blew into their mouths as they teased their mounts on.

But what?

The soldiers rode in columns of two and totalled more than eighty in number. A supply wagon brought up the rear of the column and had massive water barrels strapped to its sides. Fort Dixon had ensured that Wallis and his men were well prepared for the mission they had been given.

Wallis was a seasoned officer who had been stationed at Fort Dixon for nearly a decade. He had the reputation of being a hard man and a cruel task master, yet his men were loyal. For some men can muster loyalty in their troops by example. Wallis was such a man. They knew that he was one of that rare breed of commanding officers who led from the front.

It had been nearly three hours since the cavalry had entered the dry canyon. For all of that time, they had seen nothing living except the vultures which floated on the hot thermals above them.

For most of their number, this was the very first time that they had even come close to Devil's Pass, let alone ridden into it. Yet none of them were afraid because Captain Wallis showed no fear.

He was the yardstick by which they measured everything. As long as he remained at the head of their column, then everything ought to be OK. It was a simple logic.

The soldiers moved slowly behind Captain Wallis, who sat astride his tall grey charger. He dictated the pace and they followed. As always, they trusted the experienced officer. For he was not a man to sacrifice the lives of his enlisted men.

Sergeant Hanks spurred his weathered mount until it drew level with Wallis and then teased back on his reins. He had done the same thing countless times before on previous patrols, but for some reason, he knew that this mission was different from all the others. He could sense it.

The two horses walked side by side for more than five minutes before the officer glanced across at the red-faced Hanks. He had known the man with the mutton-chop side whiskers for his entire time at Fort Dixon. They had been on so many patrols together that they seemed to be able to read each other's minds.

'What's wrong, Hanks?' Wallis eventually asked the sergeant.

Hanks looked up at the captain.

'I reckon you ought to know what's eatin' at my craw, Captain.'

Wallis nodded. 'After all these years, I think I do.'

Hanks kept staring at the dusty trail before them. It was so bright that it hurt his eyes. It seemed that every mile that they travelled into this unholy place, the hotter it got. Sweat streamed down from beneath his hatband, burning his eyes.

'What was in them orders, sir?'

Captain Wallis raised his head and laughed.

'Curiosity killed the cat, Hanks.'

'What cat, Captain?' Hanks scratched his whiskers.

Wallis patted his breast pocket. 'My orders are for my eyes only.'

Hanks shrugged. 'Must be pretty important for us to ride into this place.'

The officer nodded. 'Damn important, Hanks.'

'We got Apache trouble?'

Wallis glanced at the trail ahead but did not respond to the question.

Hanks tried again. 'Outlaw trouble?'

Wallis glanced at the inquisitive

soldier and smiled.

'Quit while you're ahead, Hanks.'

'How far are we going into Devil's Pass, sir?'

'All the way through and then some,' Wallis replied.

Hanks felt his throat suddenly go drier than it had already been as the thought of travelling all the way through Devil's Pass filled his mind. He looked up at the face of the man who, he knew, never joked. If Wallis said that they were going straight through Devil's Pass, then that was what they were going to do.

The question was: why?

7

Time was against him. He had to find a place where he could see to all the bleeding knifewounds before he could fight again. Iron Eyes hauled the near-full bottle of whiskey from his saddle-bags and swilled a mouthful around his mouth before swallowing it. Then he poured the fiery liquor over the back of his gashed right hand and chest and stomach. The whiskey burned but he knew that it might help to slow down the bloodloss from his already emaciated body. His eyes darted all around him as if still not convinced that he had triumphed over the dead Apaches. Iron Eyes put the bottle to his lips again and then swallowed hard until only an inch of the amber liquid remained in the clear-glass bottle. He rammed the cork back into its neck and slid it into the bag that was tied behind the cantle of his saddle.

The weary ghostlike figure tightened and secured the cinch straps, then dropped the leather fender and stirrup back into place. He gripped on to the saddle horn, thrust his left boot into the stirrup and hauled himself up on to the back of the Indian pony. Its eyes flashed as the wounded bounty hunter slid his other boot-toe into the right stirrup.

Iron Eyes gritted his teeth and then looked down at his still-bleeding wounds. He knew that he would have either to find a doctor in this wilderness or try to sew up the knife wounds himself. He had a long needle and ball of catgut somewhere in one of the satchels of his bags, which he used to repair his saddle and tack with.

Then his mind drifted to the Bowie knife in his boot. He knew that if he made a campfire and heated up its blade, he could burn all the injuries into submission.

But there was no time right now. It

had taken him far longer than he had expected to remove his saddle and bags from his dead mount and transfer it to the skittish Indian pony.

Holding tightly on to his reins, he spurred the pony and rode up to the top of the high sand-dune. He stopped his mount and stared down at the trail that led from Waco. Iron Eyes squinted into the sun and knew that his pursuer had gained a lot of ground on him.

The rider was now close. Too damn close.

'Who is he?' he drawled angrily to himself. 'And what the hell is he following me for?'

The sun glinted off the unmistakable metal-tipped barrel of a rifle jutting from beneath the saddle of the powerful mount as it charged ever closer towards the bounty hunter's high vantage point atop the dune. It was a big rifle.

'What's he got there, an elephant gun?' Iron Eyes mumbled under his breath as he vainly tried to make out the man's features. Whoever he was, he did not recognize either him or his mount.

A thousand thoughts drifted through Iron Eyes's mind. Could this be Harve Calhoon? Could he have somehow managed to turn the tables on him? Turned the hunter into the hunted? Maybe it was some innocent drifter who happened to be riding the same trail as himself. Was that possible?

Suddenly, as Iron Eyes ran the fingers of his left hand through his long matted hair, he saw the rider leaning down, hauling the strange weapon from its scabbard. Before Iron Eyes had time to lower his arm he saw the plume of gunsmoke spew from the distant barrel and then heard the deafening sound echo all around him as a bullet tore into the sand at his pony's unshod hoofs.

'Buffalo gun! The bastard's got a buffalo gun!' Iron Eyes shouted at the heavens as it became obvious that whoever the rider was, the varmint wanted him dead.

Iron Eyes knew that the rider was

now probably less than fifteen minutes behind him. He had no intention of facing anyone until he had time to tend his wounds. His bony hands hauled his reins to his right.

Then he saw the faint remnants of tracks left by Harve Calhoon's horse's hoofs in the sand beyond the bodies.

Another blast filled his ears as he felt the heat of the large-calibre bullet pass within inches of his already nervous mount. Iron Eyes spurred the pony hard.

The horse did not require a reminder from the jagged edges of his sharp spurs. It thundered through the scattered bodies of the Apache warriors and across the sand. He rode the pony for all it was worth.

Now, below the crest of the dune, Iron Eyes had a little time before the unknown rider with the buffalo gun could fire at him again. The dune provided him with cover until the rider rode up and on to it.

He had maybe ten minutes before the

man reached the top of the high sandy rise and was able to take aim once more.

Iron Eyes urged the pony on and on. He had to try and get out of range of the weapon which, he knew, was capable of bringing down a fully grown buffalo at over a mile's distance.

Once the rider stopped his mount and was able to take careful aim Iron Eyes knew that he and his pony would be goners. The mysterious horseman had come close enough to his chosen target when riding at full gallop, there was no way he would miss once he had time to stop his horse.

The mount obeyed its new master and galloped towards the distant canyon. Iron Eyes stood in his stirrups and felt the pace of the pony quicken beneath him.

His keen eyes squinted into the shimmering heat haze at what was left of Calhoon's trail, but it was the man behind him who kept returning to his thoughts now.

Who was he? Iron Eyes asked himself as he balanced in his stirrups and allowed the pony beneath him its head.

But men like the infamous Iron Eyes had a thousand enemies whom they had never seen or even heard of. It came with the occupation for which he had become legendary at doing so well. Every one of the wanted men whom he had killed to claim the bounty on their heads had either a father, brother or cousin who sought revenge if they were capable.

There were thousands of outlaws' kinfolk out there who wanted to see the head of Iron Eyes on a pike.

As he galloped on Iron Eyes had no idea that he was heading straight into the jaws of a place that was probably more dangerous than any wanted outlaw or Indian whom he had ever encountered.

Iron Eyes was galloping into Devil's Pass.

8

Big Jack Brady was indeed just that. Big by any definition of the word that anyone could think of. Standing over six feet seven inches in height and weighing nearly 300 pounds, the outlaw had met few men who dared to challenge him. Those who had were all dead, either by his skilled use of the guns he wore strapped to his broad hips, or by the dozen men who trailed in his large shadow.

For more than forty years the huge outlaw had roamed steadily south from the Canadian logging camps high in the tree-covered mountains that had spawned him, until he had discovered the lands once partitioned off as the Indian territories.

But the various tribes that had been forced off their own land and brought hundreds of miles to this inhospitable terrain soon evaporated when men like Big Jack muscled their way in. The tribes that remained in the designated territory were the more hardy people such as the Apache and Comanche who were used to living on even the most arid of lands. Yet even they kept their distance from the growing outlaw population.

At first the Indians had welcomed the outlaws, but soon they discovered that their guests had only one intention, and that was to take complete control of the entire territory.

Situated on the western side of Devil's Pass, the territory soon became known simply as the Badlands. It proved to be a safe haven for the outlaws who, like Big Jack Brady, roamed the West robbing and killing. For the law never entered the Badlands. It was still officially regarded as Indian land on the maps and documents back East and therefore not subject to the laws that ruled the rest of the states. As long as the Indians remained within its boundaries and behaved themselves, the government wanted nothing to do with the place. Anyone who ventured across its borders did so at their own risk.

Money still flowed in regularly from the Federal Reserve to the half-dozen Indian agents who had remained long after their charges had left. For the unscrupulous agents were paid in gold to buy food for the thousands of Indians in their care. Having never informed the powers back East that things had changed and that they had few if any Indians to look after, the agents had grown wealthy.

A town had sprung up in the very centre of the Badlands and although it did not appear on any official maps, it was quite prosperous and popular with the outlaws who found sanctuary there.

Calico had everything that other similar-sized towns outside the notorious Badlands had, but it had more. More of everything. More saloons. More brothels. More gambling-houses.

The only thing that it had less of than the towns outside the Badlands, was law.

Even though a crude form of self-government existed in Calico to keep the thieves from stealing the gold fillings out of each others' mouths, it was not based on any known legal system. It was the law of the gun that ruled.

It was lynch law.

The strongest became even stronger.

Big Jack Brady had managed to carve himself out a tidy slice of Calico since his arrival with his henchmen. Few dared to argue with the burly man. Those who had been in Calico since it had first grown out of the dry sand resented him, but as long as he did not try to take what was theirs they tolerated his presence.

Another reason why few law-abiding people had ever heard of Calico was simple. There were only two ways into the wild town.

One route came down from the north

across almost uninhabited land, long vacated by half a dozen tribes, and the only other way to reach it was via a trail deep within the fearsome Devil's Pass.

To the thousands of outlaws and people who had made Calico their home it seemed that they had found paradise.

But they had no idea that one man in their midst had a plan that would soon put every one of them in jeopardy.

Big Jack Brady had a plan that was daring and almost as big as he was himself. If it worked he would become the most powerful individual in Calico, if it went wrong, it could bring the wrath of an entire nation down on them.

Yet men like Brady cared little for the worries of others; he thought of only himself. If Calico was destroyed by his actions, he would simply continue riding south, taking his followers, in search of another place to plunder.

Big Jack Brady had played seven hands of five-card-stud and not seen enough picture cards to make three of a kind. Yet he had won all seven hands due to the fact that his opponents knew better than to try and bluff such a huge awesome figure. Of all the saloons in Calico, the Wayward Gun was one that suited Brady and his henchmen, for it served good liquor and was filled with spineless customers. For men used to pushing their considerable weight around, it was perfect. They had taken rooms above the large sawdust-covered drinking and gambling area. The Wayward Gun was a place where a man could indulge in every known vice and that also suited Big Jack and his followers.

His hooded eyes glanced up from the card-table at the dust-caked man entering through the swing-doors. No amount of trail grime could disguise the figure of Harve Calhoon to those who knew him though.

'Harve Calhoon!' Big Jack smiled, tossed his cards on to the pile of gaming-chips and rose from his chair.

'So you finally managed to get here.'

Calhoon dusted off his Stetson against his leg and grinned at the towering figure who walked towards him, his entire entourage behind him. He knew that Big Jack was a man that you could never afford to trust, but he also paid well. The giant gunman was also someone who had a flair for devising the most outrageous robberies and bringing in experts to help him execute them. Only one thing had brought Calhoon to the Badlands and that was curiosity.

'Your plan sounded too interesting to ignore, Big Jack,' he said, rubbing the dust from his features. 'I just had to ride here to find out more.'

Brady banged the bar counter with a fist that was twice the size of any other within the building, or the town for that matter.

'A bottle of rye and two clean glasses, barkeep,' Big Jack demanded loudly.

The bottle came quickly, as did the

two thimble glasses.

Big Jack scooped them up and then led Calhoon to a quiet corner in the saloon. They sat down whilst all of Brady's men stood guard around the table.

'So ya interested, huh?' the giant man asked as he tossed the cork away and poured two full measures of the whiskey into the pair of glasses.

'Sure am. Sounds a mighty fine deal.' Calhoon nodded before tossing the drink down his parched throat. 'I figure that it must be an awful long way off, though, to pay the kinda money that you mentioned in your wire.'

'Nearer than you think, Harve.' Big Jack chuckled.

Harve Calhoon knew better than to put anything beyond this large man's capabilities. Even robbing the very town that he was holed up in.

'You ain't thinking of robbing some-one in Calico, are you?'

'Nope.' Brady grinned. 'But close, Harve. Damn close.'

Now Calhoon's curiosity was truly fired up.

'What is this job?'

'Ya understand the reason that I singled you out from the rest of your gang?' Big Jack Brady downed his drink and then poured two more.

'I reckon so, Big Jack.' Calhoon was an expert with dynamite and any other known explosive. He knew that whatever this job was it involved blowing something up. But what?

'Where are the rest of your gang?' Brady looked up at the swing-doors of the Wayward Gun as if expecting to see Calhoon's brother and men walking in after him.

'They rode on to Waco and I cut through Devil's Pass.'

The large man poured even more whiskey. 'Good. I only needed you anyway, Harve.'

Calhoon lifted the glass and studied it for a few seconds before gazing into the eyes of the man before him. They were cold, calculating eyes.

'I'm here and waiting to be told some details, Big Jack. I had me a damn tough ride just getting here.'

Big Jack nodded. 'You must be eager, Harve. You see, I needed an expert and you're it. The rest of your boys would be useless on this job.'

Calhoon downed the drink and felt the warmth starting to burn through the dust that had been choking him for his entire ride to this remote place. But he was still none the wiser as to what the large man wanted of him.

'I'm curious. What do you need a dynamite man for?'

Big Jack toyed with the glass in his hand. 'To blow something up, Harve. What else?'

'But what?'

Brady grinned broadly.

'That's something that I'll tell you tomorrow when I get the rest of the boys together.'

Harve Calhoon accepted another glass of whiskey and raised it to his dry, cracked lips. He could not imagine

74

what use his expertise with dynamite could possibly be to the gigantic man before him. But he had known Brady too many years to underestimate the man's prowess at planning and executing the most daring of robberies.

Whatever Big Jack Brady had in mind, it must be like the outlaw himself.

Big!

9

The sun was still blazing down over the sand-coloured canyon walls and filling the deep trails that wound their way tortuously through it. It was like standing inside an oven with no protection. Even the shadows seemed little cooler than the direct sunlight. The platoon were suffering and their superior officer knew it.

This was a place where things died.

He would not take risks with the lives of his men.

The troopers were gathered around the chuck wagon, drinking and eating the hastily prepared meal. Captain Wallis had decided that his men and their mounts required constant stops to fill themselves with water if they were ever to make it through Devil's Pass.

The seasoned officer leaned his rigid back against the sand-coloured rockface and stared up at the cloudless blue sky above the canyon walls and at the black-winged birds that flew in circles, watching everything in the canyon.

Wallis had never liked vultures.

Of all the deadly creatures which he had encountered upon coming westward after leaving West Point, it was the vulture that chilled him the most.

Venomous snakes and scorpions had never troubled him even though they could kill even men of Sergeant Hanks's build. There had always been something grim about the ugly birds, which were capable of tearing the flesh from anything already killed by another.

They were so lazy, and yet so majestic once airborne.

He sipped at his canteen and continued watching them floating around over the tops of the cliffs.

They were waiting.

Waiting for death to grant them another free meal.

Hanks walked up to his superior and

offered one of the tin plates of stew to him.

'Don't pay them birds no heed, sir.'

Captain Wallis accepted the plate and stared at the food upon it.

'I'd ask what this is but I think it might be wise to wait until I've eaten it, Hanks.'

Hanks lifted a spoonful of the stew up to his mouth and began chewing it. His eyebrows rose in surprise.

'It's good.'

The captain tried some, then nodded in agreement.

'I wonder what the meat in this stew is?'

'Best not be too nosy, sir. Cookie can get a tad ornery when it comes to discussing his recipes.'

Wallis continued eating.

'Do you like vultures, Hanks?'

Hanks paused his chewing.

'Ain't never tasted one, sir. Reckon this is chicken or beef, though.'

Wallis glanced at the grinning man and then back up at the circling birds.

'Don't they make you feel like they're just waiting for you to drop dead?'

'Had me a wife once who did that.' Hanks continued eating. 'That's why I enlisted. To get away from that bitch. Compared to her, them vultures are damn attractive, sir.'

Wallis looked across at his men who were watering their horses and eating. He then looked around the canyon. This was a place that he would never come within a hundred miles of if it were not for the orders in his breast pocket.

'Do you think that it's getting hotter, Hanks?' the officer scooping up another spoonful of the stew.

'Yep. Hotter than hell.'

Wallis loosened the collar stud under his sweating chin and gave a long sigh.

'I've never seen horses lather up like this when they're only walking. This place is deadly.'

'This is a dangerous place OK, sir.' Hanks finished his meal and licked the plate clean. 'Them papers must be mighty important for you to be ordered to bring us into here. I wonder why you've had to bring us here?'

'They are very important, Hanks.'

Hanks smiled and accepted the plate from the officer. 'You still ain't gonna tell me what them orders say, are you?'

'Not yet.'

'I reckon I'll have to just fret about it, then.'

Captain Wallis looked back up at the vultures.

'Tell Cookie that I enjoyed the stew and inform the men that we'll be heading on in exactly five minutes.'

'Yes, sir.' Hanks shrugged and began walking back to the chuck wagon.

10

Now the true magnitude of the canyon walls became clear to the bounty hunter. He had never ridden this way before and knew that if it were not for the tracks of Calhoon's horse in the sand before him, and the rider with the deadly buffalo gun somewhere behind him, he would not be here now. His eyes strained to see in the shimmering heat haze as he urged the terrified pony on. He could just about see what remained of the outlaw's tracks leading into the pass before him but it was the thought of becoming a target to such an ugly weapon that kept him moving forward.

Iron Eyes thundered across the hot white sand, knowing that he had to get as much distance between himself and his pursuer as possible. He had not looked behind him for more than ten minutes knowing that to even attempt to do so would slow the pace of the Indian pony beneath him.

He would find out soon enough when the hunter with the buffalo gun had reached the sandy dune. He just hoped that he would be able to outride the deadly cartridge that would seek his back.

The pony headed straight between the high canyon walls and into the wide valley. Iron Eyes whipped the shoulders of his mount with the long loose ends of his reins.

Then he heard the sound that he had dreaded.

It sounded like a thunderclap.

The echo of the shot bounced off the sand-coloured walls as he rode between them.

The buffalo gun had been fired far behind the unshod hoofs of the pony. The sound of the bullet passing within inches of him made the bounty hunter's blood boil with anger.

Who dared shoot at Iron Eyes?

As he forced his mount on to find even greater speed, he saw a huge chunk of the wall towering in front of him shatter under the impact of the large-calibre bullet.

Debris exploded into the air.

Iron Eyes hauled his reins to the side, leaned over the neck of the startled creature and spurred again. Now he turned his head and stared back at the mounted man far behind him, with the buffalo gun in his hands.

He could see the man aiming once more.

Another deafening shot cut through the hot air and hit the opposite canyon wall, showering the rider with more small fragments of rock and dust.

He galloped on with even more determination to get out of range of the gruesome weapon.

Iron Eyes knew that he was still within range of his attacker and yet luck was still on his side. So far he had managed to avoid the lethal lead twice.

The bounty hunter began to force his

pony to zigzag across the hot sand. He knew that it was far harder to hit a skilled horseman than a stationary buffalo.

Harder and harder Iron Eyes urged the pony on into the hot sun-baked pass. He knew that he had to try and cover another fifty or so yards to ensure that he was well beyond the range of the mighty gun.

But it was not so easy.

The sand beneath the Apache pony's hoofs was soft and yielding. It was not the best ground over which to maintain any speed and Iron Eyes knew that the lathered-up pony was flagging beneath him.

Then the bounty hunter felt the sheer power of another shot tearing through the flapping tails of his long trail coat. A split second later the noise of the rifle-shot erupted all around him. The force of the bullet as it hit the coat tail was powerful enough to cause the pony to stumble and make its master fight just to remain atop its back.

The pony went down on its knees.

Iron Eyes felt himself falling but grabbed at the pony's neck as the bullet struck rock a few yards ahead of him. More debris showered over him as his long legs hit the ground.

A cloud of dust rose into the air from the pony's hoofs.

For a few moments, Iron Eyes could see nothing as he clung desperately to the pony's rearing neck. For a few precious moments the bounty hunter had cover from the deadly rifle that he knew was still seeking his destruction.

As the swirling dust cleared his keen eyes spotted the distant rider once more galloping after him. Iron Eyes knew that the rifleman must have thought that he had finally hit his target.

The horseman behind him did not wish for his prey to get out of the range of his lethal weapon. He was coming in for the kill.

Whoever he was, the rider was determined to finish off Iron Eyes once and for all.

Iron Eyes knew that he only had a few seconds before his opponent realized his mistake. After steadying the frightened animal, the bounty hunter swiftly checked himself and the pony. Blood trailed down the outside of his left leg from where the bullet had torn across his thigh. The bony fingertips touched the graze.

He winced.

But it was not as bad as some of his untended wounds.

To his relief, the pony at least was unscathed.

Iron Eyes lifted the left-hand tail of his long coat. It was virtually blown away. What was left of it was little more than smouldering threads.

'Whoever you are, stranger,' Iron Eyes growled as he gathered up his reins, 'I'm gonna kill you real slow.'

He caught his breath and stepped back into his stirrup again. He mounted the pony and spurred once more. The animal thundered deeper into Devil's Pass.

He was now more than angry.

He was furious.

Even Iron Eyes did not try to shoot folks in the back, not even if they had a price on their head.

The two Navy Colts in his belt were virtually useless at this distance. He knew it was pointless even trying to shoot back at the rider with the buffalo gun. There was no way that his pistols could compete with such a formidable weapon.

But the buffalo gun had one drawback. Having such large bullets, it had to be reloaded after every shot.

As he rode on, Iron Eyes began to formulate a plan in his mind.

A plan that would require nerves of steel and perfect timing.

11

Iron Eyes noticed that the canyon pass was becoming narrower and narrower the further he rode into it. Whether this was a good or bad thing, he had no idea. The bounty hunter lashed the long ends of his reins across the bloodied shoulders of his galloping mount forcing it ever onward.

Even wounded, Iron Eyes was still a terrifying sight as he balanced in his stirrups with his long black hair flapping on the collar of his trail coat like the wings of a fleeing bat desperately seeking sanctuary.

With gritted teeth he watched as dozens of vultures swooped down the pass towards him. The great birds were travelling in the opposite direction to the bleeding rider as they caught the aroma of the eight dead bodies he had left out on the sand dunes behind him.

Iron Eyes had left them the biggest meal they had ever had in the form of the dead Apaches. The vultures would not stop feeding off the human carcasses until the bones were picked clean or coyotes drove them off.

But none of this meant anything to Iron Eyes. The sound of his mount's thundering hoofs echoed all around him yet he paid no attention to the noise.

All he could think about was finding somewhere in this godforsaken place that might allow him to take cover and ambush the man who had been trying to put a bullet in his back for the past fifteen or more minutes.

Iron Eyes spurred the horse into the sweltering sun-baked pass and knew that this place was not designed to protect the hunted, only the hunter. Its smooth towering walls had little shape to them and that troubled the bounty hunter.

If he stopped his horse, he knew that he could not climb the canyon walls.

Nobody could. They were just too smooth. It was as if nature itself had sanded them down.

Iron Eyes needed a corner, a jagged boulder or anything that might be large enough to shield himself and his mount from the deadly buffalo gun.

He thundered on.

There had to be a place where he could dismount and wait for the rider to get within the range of his deadly Navy Colts, he kept telling himself.

Yet the further he rode, the less he began to believe that such a place existed within this canyon pass. For this place was unlike any other he had ever ridden through. Sweat was now pouring off the pony and himself.

He had never known anywhere to be as hot as this pass.

Iron Eyes continued to whip the now spent pony onward with even more urgency. He glanced down at his chest. His shirt and skin were covered in the blood that was still seeping from the knife wounds. His left pants leg was now also soaked in blood. He was bleeding like a stuck pig and knew he had to find somewhere to try and stem the flow of blood real fast.

Then his keen eyes spotted the thing he had been looking for, a hundred or more yards ahead of him. Iron Eyes aimed the nose of his mount towards it.

He hauled his reins to his blood-soaked chest and jumped from the back of the exhausted mount. A cloud of choking dust rose into the air and covered both man and beast for a few moments as the bounty hunter caught his breath.

Iron Eyes held firmly on to his reins and stared at the sight before him. He then convinced himself that it was real and not a mirage created by the blood-loss or unbearable heat.

It was really there.

A large rock twice his own height was propped against the canyon wall. It must have fallen from high above to the canyon floor where it now lay, he concluded. For it was different from the smooth walls of sand-coloured stone that made up the length of the trail he had ridden through so far.

He looked up and stared at the top of the high canyon. His steel-coloured eyes surveyed the entire length of it until he saw the slight blemish on an otherwise perfect surface. That was where the boulder had fallen from, he concluded.

For a few moments Iron Eyes stood perfectly still and listened. If the rider who was after him had already entered the pass he would have heard the sound of his horse's hoofs echoing by now.

There was no noise.

That meant the rider had yet to enter this devilish place.

He still had time to put his plan into action.

Iron Eyes led the pony behind the boulder and tied the reins firmly to a small jagged edge at its base. He then hauled the large water bag that he had confiscated from one of the other Apache mounts off the saddle horn and pulled out its crude stopper.

He lifted the bag to his cracked lips and swallowed two large mouthfuls of the cool liquid. It felt good as it made its way through his thin body.

Then he looked at the pony beside him.

Iron Eyes knew that he needed this pathetic animal to get him out of this place. He removed his coat and laid it down on the ground before the pony's front legs and poured a couple of pints of the precious liquid on to it.

He watched as the grateful horse drank the water. Then he hung the bag back on the saddle horn again.

Iron Eyes hauled his weapons from his belt, cocked their hammers and leaned against the large rock. He wanted to kill this man more than he had ever wanted to kill anyone.

Even if there was no price on his pursuer's head, he wanted to kill him.

There was still no noise in the pass.

All Iron Eyes could hear was the

sound of the pony behind him breathing heavily as it tried desperately to recover from the long hard ride its new master had inflicted upon it.

Iron Eyes wanted to hear the sound of his pursuer's horse galloping towards him. He craved it like a mountain lion craves the taste of fresh meat.

The pony snorted. He turned to look at it and noticed its ears prick forward. It had heard something his ears could not make out.

Iron Eyes turned back and looked down the pass to where the dust that his pony had kicked up as they had galloped to this spot still hung on the hot air.

He dropped on to the ground, pulled his long black hair away from the side of his head, and then pressed his ear to the sand.

It sounded like a heart beating.

Iron Eyes could hear the approaching horse's hoofs but they seemed slower than he expected. The rider with the buffalo gun had slowed his mount to a mere canter as he trailed the bounty hunter in Devil's Pass.

Slowly he raised his head off the sand. Iron Eyes got back to his feet and knew that he might have a much longer wait than he had at first considered.

His pursuer was smart and cautious.

This was not going to be as easy as he had planned.

He knew that the man who chased him might spot the boulder before he was in range of Iron Eyes's Navy Colts.

The bounty hunter picked his still-damp coat up off the ground and then searched its pockets for a cigar amongst the scores of bullets.

His thin fingers found a twisted half-smoked cigar. He rammed it between his teeth. He then located his matches and dragged one along the boulder.

He cupped the flame in the palms of his hands and sucked in the acrid smoke.

For a brief few seconds as he held the smoke in his lungs, he could no longer feel the pain that racked his body.

Then as he exhaled he heard the sound of the rider's horse growing louder. Suddenly he realized that he had to do something that this man would never expect him to do, if he were going to survive.

'Keep on coming, *amigo*,' Iron Eyes mumbled as he pulled his Bowie knife from his mule-ear boot and stared at its bloodstained blade. 'Iron Eyes ain't finished yet.'

12

Devil's Pass was virtually silent as the man reined in his lathered-up mount. It had taken the cautious rider with the buffalo gun perched on his hip nearly twenty minutes to reach the spot where he could see the huge boulder jutting out of the soft sand.

Something was seriously wrong and the horseman was alert enough to sense it.

But what?

Every sinew in his aching body told him that this was not going to be as simple as he had first thought when he had trailed Iron Eyes into Devil's Pass. He ran the back of his hand across his dry mouth.

The brilliant sun was no longer directly over the the pass and shadows bathed one side of the high canyon walls as the horseman steadied his restless mount. For the first time since he had started following the tall bounty hunter, he was nervous.

His mind raced.

Was this a trap?

Had Iron Eyes lured him to this place to bushwhack him? The rider sat silently in his saddle as his suspicious eyes weighed up the situation before him.

To the naïve observer, it would have seemed that there was nothing wrong. But this rider was far from naïve. He could feel the danger that lurked a couple of hundred yards ahead of him in the shimmering heat and taunting shadows.

Iron Eyes was not a man who would be easily killed, and the horseman was well aware of that chilling fact.

His finger continually stroked the large trigger of the buffalo gun as his eyes sought out the bounty hunter. The rider's attention kept returning to the huge boulder and he wondered whether his prey was behind its granite bulk. He tapped his spurs gently and allowed his horse to move forward slowly.

Then he reined in again and listened.

He was scared.

All he required was a mere glimpse of Iron Eyes and he would unleash the fury of the deadly rifle. He knew that not even the legendary bounty hunter could survive being hit by one of the buffalo gun's bullets.

He focused on the boulder, which was now half in shadow.

Was Iron Eyes hiding behind it?

Cautiously, the rider lifted his right leg over the neck of his mount and slid to the ground. The sand was soft beneath his high-heeled boots.

He held the huge weapon in both hands and walked beside his horse towards the boulder. Every few steps, the man stopped and tried to see if his quarry was hiding behind the big chunk of rock.

The shimmering heat haze that rose off the soft white sand, together with the lengthening shadows, began to play tricks on his tired eyes.

He held the buffalo gun ahead of him and carefully edged his way closer and closer to the boulder.

Sweat was now pouring down the hunter's spine beneath his shirt. This was a game that he had no experience of. This was not the way he had planned it.

This was getting complicated.

Was this a cunning trick created by the devilish Iron Eyes, or was he allowing his own vivid imagination to get the better of him?

One mistake now could prove fatal.

He was determined not to make that mistake. All he wanted to do was get one clean shot at the infamous Iron Eyes and cut him in half with his lethal weapon.

For revenge was the one thing that had driven the man onward for the previous three years in his relentless search for the man who was known as the living ghost. It was all the rider had thought about since his outlaw brother had fallen victim to the bounty hunter's deadly Navy Colts.

Vengeance meant an eye for an eye in this man's mind, and he had travelled a long way to claim this God-given right. Yet he could not take his eyes off the towering boulder before him, for he knew that death might be waiting just behind it.

His death!

This was not the way he had thought it would be. With every step, he began to feel that he had somehow stumbled into a web of Iron Eyes' design.

And he was the fly in that web.

He knew that he was still way beyond the range of Iron Eyes' Navy Colts and he intended to keep that advantage if possible.

He moved to his right and crouched against the canyon wall. He caught a glimpse of something moving behind the boulder through a two-foot gap at its base. Then he heard the distinctive sound of spurs softly echoing off the canyon walls beyond the massive rock.

'Iron Eyes!' the man whispered excitedly to himself as he felt a sense of relief filling him. The bounty hunter was lying in wait for him. He had been right to be cautious.

His right thumb pulled back on the hammer of the hefty weapon until it locked fully into position. He knew that he had to try and make the bounty hunter show himself if he were going to be able to blast him into Hell.

Then the unmistakable jangling of spurs rang out again around the canyon, sending a chill up his spine. Every muscle in his body told him that the elusive Iron Eyes was there OK. Just beyond that lump of taunting rock.

He had to outwit the bounty hunter, even if it were only for a split second. All he needed was the time it would take to aim and fire. The buffalo gun would do the rest.

The man looked at his horse and then back at the boulder. An idea began to hatch in his fevered brain.

Could Iron Eyes be distracted if he

were to send his horse galloping down the canyon past the boulder? Would the ruthless bounty hunter be drawn out from the impenetrable cover of the the large rock just long enough for the gunman to get a target?

There was only one way to find out.

He stood to his full height and then kicked the rear of the animal as hard as he could. The horse raced down the narrow canyon towards the boulder, making an awful lot of noise as it did so.

Without a moment's hesitation, the man ran behind his spooked horse with the primed buffalo gun gripped firmly in his hands. The dust that kicked up by the hoofs of his mount gave him a little cover and he intended to use that to his advantage. As he got closer to the huge boulder his eyes were locked on to the gap between it and the rockface.

His squinting eyes could clearly see movement beyond its huge bulk. Shadows danced on the canyon wall.

The low-life Iron Eyes was hiding

there, waiting to ambush him, he thought.

His horse had only just passed the boulder when it slowed to a halt, then turned to look at whatever was hiding behind the large rock. It too had seen something behind the boulder, the man told himself.

The man was now within the range of the Navy Colts. He had to act quickly if he were to survive a showdown with such a devious and skilled enemy. He would have to get a clean shot with his buffalo gun to finish the bounty hunter off with one bullet. The man knew that he would have little time to reload the mighty single-shot rifle in his hands if he missed his target.

It was a thought too awesome to even dwell upon.

This had to be done swiftly.

He crouched into the floating dust and then ran to the opposite rockface. He could see the Apache pony clearly just behind the rock as it vainly fought against its bonds.

Where was Iron Eyes?

Knowing that he was risking walking into the deadly sights of Iron Eyes' Navy Colts, he trained the barrel of his buffalo gun in the direction of the skittish pony and cautiously edged forward.

Inch by inch, his boots moved along the canyon wall through the soft sand.

Sweat poured from beneath his Stetson hatband and ran unchecked down his weathered face.

Then he caught sight of the bounty hunter's long trail coat against the boulder and the distinctive blue gun resting by its frayed sleeve-cuff halfway up the jagged rock.

A sense of panic suddenly overwhelmed him.

The long trail coat was covered in blood and Iron Eyes was motionless. A thousand questions raced unanswered inside the sniper's brain. Had Iron Eyes died from the shot that had brought him off his pony earlier?

With a speed that defied the heat of Devil's Pass, he ran forward and squeezed the trigger. The buffalo gun blasted its deafening charge. The bullet hit the coat dead centre and the boulder exploded into a thousand pieces.

The man watched it fall to the ground.

His eyes widened when he realized that the trail coat had been carefully placed against the side of the boulder. There was no one inside it's already blood-soaked fabric.

Where was Iron Eyes? His mind screamed as his fingers desperately pulled another bullet from the belt hanging over his shoulder. He opened the chamber of the weapon, pulled out the still-smoking brass casing, then slid the fresh shell into the chamber. He locked it into place.

Then he heard the sound of spurs again.

He hauled the hefty weapon around and stared at the spurs hanging on the saddle horn of the terrified Indian pony.

'What the hell?' he muttered as the thought that he had been well and truly tricked sank at last into his fevered brain.

He stared at the coat on the ground, then searched the area behind the boulder for the man he was hunting. There was no sign of Iron Eyes anywhere.

Had the bounty hunter somehow disappeared into thin air?

That was the way it seemed to the confused man as he lowered the rifle and moved towards the tethered Indian pony and the long sharp spurs that had been deliberately left hanging on the saddle horn.

Before he had time to think, he heard a sudden noise behind him. He twisted on his heels and fired his buffalo gun again.

Blood splattered all over him.

He watched in horror as his horse was nearly cut in half by the shot from his own smoking weapon. The pitiful creature was knocked backwards and crumpled heavily into the blood-covered sand.

His startled gaze darted away from the body of the stricken animal and began searching the canyon for the bounty hunter, who had disappeared.

Would Iron Eyes have abandoned his mount and chosen to flee this deadly place on foot? The large water bag was still hanging from the saddle horn next to the spurs. It seemed ridiculous to even consider that any sane man would choose to leave his pony and the bag full of precious water, but was the bounty hunter sane?

The frightened man knew little of the prey whom he had hunted for so many years, except that Iron Eyes killed mercilessly, and without regret.

Before he could move a muscle he caught sight of something out of the corner of his eye on the white sand. At first he thought that it might be a sidewinder or a lizard. His head turned and his jaw dropped as he focused on the sand to his left.

He began to shake.

Slowly, Iron Eyes rose out of the soft white sand with one of his Navy Colts gripped firmly in his bony right hand.

'Lookin' for me, mister?' the bounty hunter asked.

The man stared at the ghostly apparition as the voice echoed all about him. He had heard many voices in his lifetime but none that sounded like this one.

His wrinkled eyes widened at the startling sight of the figure that rose out of the shallow sandy grave before him with the cocked pistol in his hand. He had not even considered that the bounty hunter would use the long blade of his Bowie knife to dig a shallow trench in which to bury himself, to wait patiently for the hunter to get within the range of his pistol.

For a moment the man could not believe the gruesome vision that he was witnessing. For the white sand had stuck to the blood-soaked bounty hunter, making him appear like a zombie rising from its grave.

'What the hell?' he croaked as he hastily reloaded the buffalo gun in his shaking hands.

Iron Eyes did not wait for the man to aim the buffalo gun once more. He fired the Navy Colt, then cocked its hammer again and fired again.

The wide-eyed man went flying backwards and hit the canyon wall hard. He slid slowly down its smooth surface leaving a trail of crimson gore behind him until he stopped in a sitting position a score of feet from the smoking barrel of the Navy Colt.

Iron Eyes staggered to his feet. He walked towards the body and kicked the rifle out of its lifeless hands. He then tore the hat from the head and looked hard at the unseeing face.

He did not recognize his pursuer.

The bony fingers searched the pockets of the dead man but they could not find anything that gave a clue as to his identity. All Iron Eyes knew for sure was that this man had hurt him real bad. He knew that there were many men like this one, who wanted to settle a score with the ruthless bounty hunter who had so cold-bloodedly claimed the lives of their loved ones.

Iron Eyes lifted his other Navy Colt off the boulder, tucked it into his belt next to its still-hot twin and spat at the body at his feet. He then paused and stared at the dead face again.

The eyes of the dead man were still wide open. Iron Eyes lifted what was left of his trail coat off the sand and studied the damage the buffalo gun had done to it. It was the worse for wear and full of holes of various sizes but there was still enough of it left to wear, he thought.

He slipped it on.

As he pulled his mount away from the corpse, Iron Eyes hauled the whiskey bottle from the saddle-bag, swilled what was left of the liquor around his teeth, then swallowed. He tossed the bottle away, grabbed the head of the pony and whispered into its ear.

'He looks as if he seen a ghost,' he said, looking at the open eyes of the dead man.

The bounty hunter mounted and tapped his mule-ear boots into the flesh of the still nervous pony. It responded and began to canter. A few yards beyond the dead horse he saw the hooftracks left in the sand by Harve Calhoon.

Iron Eyes continued tracking the outlaw.

13

Captain Hugh Wallis reined in his powerful mount. The sound of the buffalo gun still resounded all about him and his platoon of weary troopers. At first it had sounded to the horseman like a distant thunderclap, until his ears heard the rest of the brief battle echoing around them.

It had been a long time since he had heard the unmistakable sound of a buffalo gun being fired. It had once been a common noise on the Plains until the vast herds of nomadic buffalo disappeared.

The experienced officer held his mount firmly in check with both his white-gauntleted hands. He looked behind him at the troubled faces of his men as their eyes vainly searched the walls of the pass for a hint of where the shots had come from.

Wallis signalled to Hanks.

Hanks rode along the line of horsemen until he reached Wallis's side then he dragged his reins up to his chest and pushed his battered cavalry hat off his tanned brow.

'What in tarnation was that, sir?' Hanks asked anxiously. 'Dynamite?'

Wallis inhaled deeply and then heard the echoes of the fainter sound of the Navy Colt also bouncing off the high canyon walls.

'That was not dynamite, Hanks. But maybe something almost as destructive.' The officer sighed.

The sergeant looked hard at the captain. 'What in tarnation is anywhere as destructive as dynamite, sir?'

The officer's eyes flashed at Hanks.

'A buffalo gun, Hanks! A buffalo gun!'

Hanks steadied his horse. 'A buffalo gun?'

Wallis nodded.

'And a handgun. It seems to me that someone along the trail has been having themselves an old-fashioned shootout by the sounds of it, Hanks.'

Hanks scratched his sidewhiskers.

'But who on earth would have a buffalo gun nowadays? It must be five years since the last buffalo was seen around here.'

Wallis had no answers.

'Maybe we ought to try and find out. Get Billy Bodine,' he ordered.

Hanks stood in his stirrups and called back at the two columns of troopers for the young corporal, who was renowned for his horsemanship. It did not take long for the trooper to make himself seen as he steered his magnificent chestnut quarter horse from next to the distant chuck wagon and headed for the shouting sergeant. Bodine galloped through the long, darkening shadows past the eighty cavalrymen until he reached the two riders at the head of the column.

Billy Bodine had enlisted a year earlier and had quickly gained promotion, mainly due to his skill atop a horse. He was fearless and had never once hesitated to obey an order however dangerous it might be.

'Howdy, Captain.' Bodine smiled as he ran his gloved hand along the neck of his mount. 'Reckon you must want me to go scouting for you?'

Wallis tried not to show his amusement at the youngster's total inability to be browbeaten by any man whatever his rank.

'Correct, Billy. I want you to ride that fine animal of yours up this canyon to try and find out who is doing all the shooting.'

Bodine looked happy as he gathered his reins together in one hand.

'You want me join in the fight, Captain? If'n they start shooting at me?'

'No. Just check it out and then get back here as fast as you can and let me know what you find out.' Wallis sighed. 'I don't want to lead the platoon into a bloodbath.'

'Could be Indians up there, sir,'

Hanks said thoughtfully.

'Possibly. We are close to the Indian territories.' Wallis nodded knowingly. 'But it seems doubtful that they would have a buffalo gun.'

'What if it is Indians, Captain?' Bodine queried. 'Should I keep my distance?'

'I'll leave that up to your judgement, Billy. Just don't bring a whole bunch of them on your heels when you return back here. I'm in no mood to fight Indians.'

Billy Bodine gave out a yell that alerted his highly strung quarter horse to start running.

Wallis and Hanks watched as the skilled young trooper thundered away from them into the distance. Neither man had ever seen anyone who could ride as well as Bodine. He seemed to be part of the horse that he rode.

'A fine young man,' Wallis said.

'Yep. A real horseman.' Hanks agreed.

The officer looked up at the darkening sky above the tops of the canyon walls. He knew that they ought to make camp again but something told him that the time was not quite right. He could sense danger this night and knew that it was far wiser to keep his men in the saddle.

'What you thinking about, sir?' Hanks asked.

'I'm thinking that we should continue along the pass for the time being, Hanks,' Captain Wallis replied.

The sergeant knew exactly what the seasoned campaigner was thinking about. He wanted to venture deeper into Devil's Pass whilst the sun was off the men behind them.

'I'll inform the men, sir.'

Wallis reached across to the veteran sergeant's shoulder and cleared his throat.

'Wait a few minutes, Hanks.'

Hanks held his mount in check. 'Sir?'

Wallis removed one of his gauntlets, then unbuttoned his breast pocket. He pulled out the two folded sheets of paper and handed them to the surprised rider.

'I thought that you might wish to read the orders first.'

Hanks gave a wry smile and unfolded the papers.

'About time, sir.'

Wallis did not reply. He had too much weighing on his mind to say another word until his second-in-command knew why they were in this unholy place. He watched Hanks reading and then stared at the dust still hanging in the hot air. Dust that had been kicked up off the hoofs of Bodine's galloping mount.

He wondered how eager the sergeant would be to continue once he had read the orders.

14

It had been dark for a couple of hours but Calico was no cooler than it had been when the sun had been blazing down on its wooden buildings. The rooms above the Wayward Gun saloon were nothing more than practical. A bed and a chair plus a small dresser with a jug of water and a bowl on its top were all you got for five dollars a night, but most who spent time within the small square rooms were grateful just to have a roof above their heads for a change.

Harve Calhoon had been surprised when Big Jack Brady had knocked heavily on the door of his hotel room. The low booming voice was unmistakable, though, as it instructed the outlaw to join him and the rest of his men downstairs in the back room.

'OK, Big Jack,' Calhoon shouted at

the locked door.

Calhoon heard the heavy footsteps walking back along the passage away from his room before he lowered his legs from his bed to the floor. He was tired and wanted to sleep but knew that Brady was not the sort of man you ignored.

He stared out of the window at the rising moon, then hauled his boots on over his worn socks. He was beginning to worry about why Brady needed a dynamite expert in the first place.

What was the giant man planning?

A bank robbery?

It had to be something as big as the man himself.

He rubbed his weary face, trying to wake himself up. Then his thoughts focused on Brady again. What did he want? There seemed no reason why the large outlaw would need to talk to him now, he thought. It had already been agreed that Brady would not reveal his plans to his assembled team until the following day.

Calhoon stood, lifted his gunbelt off the brass bedpost, strapped it around his hips and buckled it up. His skilled fingers instinctively confirmed that it was loaded and ready for action.

Even now he did not trust Brady. Some things just did not add up but he could not think why. The Calhoon gang had always made sure that they did not take on a job which was beyond their capabilities. Harve Calhoon wondered if he was up to the task that Brady had conceived in his fertile imagination.

The outlaw walked slowly to the small dresser and poured cold water from the large white jug into the basin. He splashed it over his face and hair. He ran his fingers through his hair, then dried his face with the tail of his bandanna. He was little more than half-awake when he unlocked the door, walked along the dimly lit passage and descended the flight of stairs into the large room where men were still drinking and gambling and females were still plying for trade.

He walked to the back of the building and saw the dozen or more men gathered in the rear room of the saloon. Big Jack Brady raised a hand and signalled for him to join them. The outlaw obeyed. He felt uneasy even though he recognized half the faces within the room gathered around Big Jack Brady.

Something was just not right.

He tried not to yawn as Brady gestured to an empty chair next to him at the large circular table.

'Now we can start, boys,' Brady announced to the gathered assembly of equally stunned and confused outlaws.

Calhoon rubbed his face with both his hands and glanced at the larger man.

'What are you talking about, Big Jack?'

Brady grinned. It was like the man himself. Big.

'I kinda hoodwinked you earlier,' he told Calhoon. 'You see, I've been hoping that you would turn up today because it makes the whole job a lot easier. I had the other boys all stashed away in other hotels and saloons around Calico for the last few days but without you, Harve, we could not act.'

'I don't understand, Big Jack.' Calhoon sighed. 'If you were waiting for me before you could get this job rolling, why didn't you tell me earlier?'

'Because you were not the final piece in the jigsaw,' Brady answered, 'but you are the most important.'

Harve Calhoon was still no wiser. 'What the hell are you talking about?'

Brady pointed across the table at a small man who resembled a lizard. Calhoon looked at the skittish man but did not recognize him.

'This, gentlemen, is Black Roy Hart. He's the final piece of my jigsaw puzzle. He only arrived in town an hour or so back and he brought the ingredients to enable us to accomplish the job that I've been planning for the last six months.'

Calhoon stared at the unsmiling Hart.

'What did you bring that's so darn important, Black Roy?'

'Dynamite sticks and all,' Hart replied.

'We had the dynamite man but not the dynamite itself, Harve.' Brady pulled out a scrap of paper from his vest pocket and laid it on the table. He unfolded it and every eye around the room stared at the seemingly meaningless hand-drawn map.

'But I got me some dynamite in my saddle-bags,' Calhoon said. Big Jack laughed. 'Not enough, Harve. This is a real big job and needs a real lot of dynamite.'

'How much?'

'A wagonload, boy,' came the reply.

Calhoon looked around the table and began to recognize the faces of some of the other outlaws. Each was an expert in his own field and slowly Calhoon began to understand the enormity of what Brady had planned. Anything that required such a prodigious amount of explosives had to be beyond anything he had ever tackled before.

'What did you mean when you said that you were glad that I turned up today and not in a couple of days' time, Big Jack?' he asked.

Brady tilted his enormous head.

'Now we can ride tonight and get this job done. If you had been a tad slower reaching Calico, we would have had to wait for another three months.'

Harve Calhoon frowned.

'What is this job?'

Big Jack Brady turned the scrap of paper around and pointed to the crude drawings. He watched as Calhoon's eyes looked down at the place at which the finger was aimed. A picture of a train and a long, sturdy wooden bridge spanning a wide valley seemed to jump out at the still-tired outlaw.

Calhoon looked up at the face of the man beside him.

'You want me to blow up a train?'

Brady shook his head.

'Not the train. The bridge! You gotta blow up that bridge so the train has to stop and when it stops, we attack it, kill every critter that stands in our way and then take three months' worth of gold coin headed for Fort Dixon.'

'The army payroll?' Calhoon queried.

'Yep. The army payroll. All three months of it. Do you have any idea how much that is, Harve?'

'Nope.'

'Well there are more than six hundred troopers at Fort Dixon.' Brady grinned. 'So it's one hell of a lot of money and no mistake. Equal shares. It could run to thousands of dollars each.'

The price was right but Calhoon wondered if he were good enough to accomplish what Brady had planned. How big was this bridge in reality? The simple pencil sketch gave no clue as to the true dimensions of the actual bridge itself.

How did you blow up an entire bridge? Sweat began to run down the side of the outlaw's face.

Harve Calhoon rubbed his dry mouth and accepted the glass of rye that was offered to him. He downed it in one swallow and exhaled loudly.

'So I'm to blow up this bridge so that you and the rest of the boys can rob the train?'

Big Jack Brady slapped Calhoon's back and roared with laughter.

'Now you getting your brain working, Harve. That's exactly right, boy. See how important you are?'

'How far away from here is it?'

'A few hours' ride north at a place called Honcho Wells,' Brady replied. 'The railtracks cut through the top of the Indian territory boundaries. The bridge spans a river.'

'Ain't that a mite close to Calico, Big Jack?' one of the other men asked. 'The army will track us back here looking for their gold.'

'Let them,' Brady scoffed. 'We'll be long gone by the time they reach Calico.'

'When's the train due?' Black Roy asked.

'It ought to reach the viaduct at Honcho Wells at noon tomorrow, give or take an hour,' Brady replied. 'I've been keepin' tabs on it for the past year.'

'Is it heavily guarded?' another of the men enquired.

'Nope. Never has more than a dozen troopers guardin' it and they're all in the car ahead of the one with the gold.'

'Like takin' candy from a baby,' Black Roy muttered.

Harve Calhoon felt a sudden chill overwhelm him as every one of the other outlaws began to chuckle along with the big man.

'And when do we do this?' he asked.

'My personal associates are getting the horses and dynamite wagon ready as we speak, Harve.' Big Jack Brady grinned. 'We ride in about ten minutes.'

Calhoon pushed his empty glass towards the whiskey bottle. He needed another drink.

15

There were several smaller trails split-
ting off from the main canyon which
were collectively known as the merciless
Devil's Pass. Yet Billy Bodine galloped
on through the narrow moonlit canyon
without taking his eyes off what lay
directly ahead of him. His instincts told
him that whatever he was looking for
was somewhere ahead. Somewhere on
the soft sand that sparkled in the bluish
light of the large moon directly
overhead.

Bodine leaned over the neck of his
charging mount as the horse continued
to gather pace.

The only sound within Devil's Pass
was the noise of his own mount. It
echoed all around the young trooper.
He had never known any place so
frightening or unholy. It troubled him
as he urged the chestnut on. Every hair

on the nape of his neck felt as if it were standing on end beneath his yellow bandanna.

His hands gripped the reins tightly as he listened to the horse's hoofs pounding across the surface of the soft sand.

To Billy Bodine it began to sound like the beating of war drums.

Were there any other living creatures in this place, Bodine asked himself. If so, where were they?

It would only take another few seconds before he knew the answer.

The powerful horse thundered around a bend. Suddenly its rider leant back on his saddle and hauled the mount to an abrupt halt.

Bodine wrestled with his reins and stood in his stirrups. His keen young eyes spotted something a few dozen yards ahead and he hauled the quarter horse around full circle while he tried to work out what it was that was lying in the centre of the sandy trail.

Whatever it was, he thought, it was dead.

The skilful horseman quickly dismounted and flicked the leather pistol flap up on his belt. He withdrew his service pistol from the holster and cocked its trigger.

Bodine held firmly on to his reins and studied the sight carefully before he led the nervous horse towards a large boulder. His mount could smell the stench of death hanging in the hot canyon.

What was left of the dead horse had already gone rigid in the intense heat that still filled Devil's Pass. As Bodine got closer, Bodine could smell the flesh already beginning to rot as he walked his horse past the carcass.

The moonlight did not make the sight any less ugly.

Then Bodine's attention was drawn to the dark shadow beside the boulder. For a moment he hesitated, then he aimed his pistol in the direction of the shadow. It soon became apparent that he did not need his weapon.

He stared down at the dead man seated where Iron Eyes had left him. It was a chilling sight.

The body was still propped up against the canyon wall staring blindly into hell itself.

Bodine looked all around him for any sign of the victor in this battle. There was no one else to be seen.

The corporal suddenly felt very afraid.

The two bullet holes were clearly visible when Bodine crouched down beside the body. Two clean shots in the centre of the dead man's chest.

Whoever had done this was good, he thought. Darn good.

Bodine looked around and then spotted the large buffalo gun lying in the soft sand. He plucked it up and checked it carefully.

To his utter surprise, he found that the lethal weapon was still loaded.

Billy Bodine holstered his own pistol and then turned to his horse. He jumped up into the air. His left boot entered the stirrup, he threw his right leg over the army saddle and then laid the buffalo gun across his lap.

Billy Bodine's imagination began to race. He sat silently atop his horse and held the reins in check. His eyes scoured the area around his nervous mount. Even the eerie moonlight could not disguise the horror that lay all around him. Bodine knew that he had to get back to the rest of the platoon and inform them of his grisly discovery. He dragged his reins hard to the right and spurred his mount.

The chestnut galloped back in the direction of the rest of Captain Wallis's men. Bodine knew that he would have to ride his mount as he had never done before if he were to alert his comrades of what he had found before sunrise. He was alone and scared.

Where was the man who had created this bloodbath? Or was this the work of something less than human?

The cavalryman thundered along the pass knowing that he too might fall victim to the same fate as the body behind him.

Then suddenly, as his mount was almost at full flight, he spotted something ahead of him on his left. He pulled back on the reins and slowed the chestnut to a halt. The horse responded immediately and allowed its master to stare into the eerie moonlight.

Bodine squinted into the half-light at the trail, which led into a small canyon pass. It was a narrow route, no more than eight feet wide; a trail that he had not spotted when he had been riding in the opposite direction.

He looked at the ground and then saw two distinctive sets of hoof-tracks in the otherwise undisturbed sand.

Bodine dismounted and knelt.

He could tell that two horses had ridden up this trail recently.

One was a shod horse and the other unshod.

Could old Hanks have been correct? Could it have been an Indian who had killed the man back at the boulder? He had heard a thousand tales of the horrors that the Apaches had inflicted on their enemies.

To the youthful horseman, they were all true.

Although he had found evidence of only one unshod pony, he allowed his fertile imagination to run unchecked.

Where there was one Apache, there had to be an entire tribe of them. This could be the beginning of another Indian War. After all, Devil's Pass was close to the Indian Territory and who knew what other barbaric acts of carnage went on there?

It was a terrified Billy Bodine who threw himself back on to his saddle and allowed the horse to continue to race along the main pass.

This was important.

There could be an entire war party of hundreds of warriors waiting for Wallis and his men, hidden in the canyons of this unholy place, he concluded.

He had to inform Captain Wallis about it.

16

The bounty hunter stared hard at the town bathed in moonlight before him. He knew that it should not be there, but it was there. Calico was strangely quiet as Iron Eyes steered the exhausted mount towards it. He could hear music playing somewhere in the heart of the town, but there were few people on the streets. The rider was totally confused. He had completely lost track of time as he had followed Harve Calhoon's hoof-tracks through the narrow maze of canyons. Now Iron Eyes was starting to doubt his own sanity as he focused on the wooden buildings ahead of him.

Was he dreaming?

Perhaps it was the blood loss that he had suffered from the knife wounds inflicted on him during the valiant battle with the Apache warrior, that was playing tricks on his weary mind.

Whatever it was, he was confused.

He was also thirsty.

He needed whiskey real bad.

Iron Eyes eased back on his reins, stopped the pony and then stared at the town again.

For a few moments he was totally baffled.

Where was he?

The bounty hunter had thought that he was heading for the Indian Territory. Yet he was looking straight at dozens of wooden buildings where there should not be a single one.

Where was this place?

Iron Eyes tried to fathom out what had happened. Had he somehow got lost and ridden into a place that he did not know existed? Could he have succumbed to the effects of his injuries and lost consciousness long enough for his pony to have ridden so far off course?

He looked down at the sand and saw the tracks of Calhoon's horse. He had trailed the man to this place, exactly as he had thought.

Another thought entered his mind.

Iron Eyes knew that he had lost an awful lot of blood during the hot afternoon, but had he lost so much that his mind was creating hallucinations?

He leaned back in his saddle and stared down at his sand-caked chest and stomach. The sand had stopped the blood flowing from his wounds but he hurt like a thousand rattlesnake bites.

'This is real,' Iron Eyes growled to himself.

He rubbed his throat.

It was dry, but he did not want to quench his thirst with water.

Iron Eyes needed whiskey to wash the dust out of his mouth and throat. He needed to burn the pain out of his body and knew that only hard liquor could do that. His keen eyes could make out at least three signs ahead of him which had the word 'saloon' painted on them.

Yet as far as he could see, there were no signs declaring the word 'sheriff'.

Iron Eyes wondered why not. Of all the hundreds of towns that he had ever ridden into over his long life as a bounty hunter, he had never once entered a town where there was no sheriff's office.

Maybe it was tucked away around a corner or in a side street, he thought. He would have to find it if he caught up with the last of the Calhoon gang, if he were to collect the bounty on the outlaw's head.

Iron Eyes knew that all towns had a sheriff's office. Just as they always had barber shops and undertakers.

But he did not dismiss his concerns totally.

He pulled one of his Navy Colts from his belt and emptied the spent bullets from it on to the sand beside his pony. His thin bony hand reached down into his deep coat pocket and gathered six bullets up. He pushed them into the chambers of his weapon and then snapped it shut. He repeated the action with his other pistol, then pushed them

140

into his belt. Both gun grips jutted out from his waist.

Whatever doubts filled his tired brain the overwhelming thirst that burned his throat persuaded him to continue.

The bounty hunter gritted his teeth and then allowed the pony to walk on. He watched every structure as he rode closer and closer to the outskirts of the town.

A crude sign informed him that this was Calico.

The name meant nothing to him.

Iron Eyes leaned down from his saddle and touched the wooden sign. It was real and so was the town itself. This was no mirage.

It actually existed.

The Indian pony approached the closest of the saloons and he hauled back on his reins. He stared up at the large sign nailed to the balcony rail above him.

The Wayward Gun Saloon.

The bounty hunter could smell the aroma of whiskey floating on the warm evening air. He dismounted slowly, wrapped his reins around the hitching pole and tied them tightly. He still did not trust the skittish animal. He knew that given half a chance, it would gallop away from its new master, taking his saddle and bags with it.

He opened one of the saddle-bags' flaps and pulled out a bag of golden eagles. He then dropped the fist-sized bag into one of his deep trail-coat pockets.

Iron Eyes stepped up on to the boardwalk and gazed over the swing doors at the gathering inside. An annoying tinny piano was being played in a corner whilst a dozen men were scattered around the large interior drinking and gambling. A few bar girls were still trying to encourage the less than sober men to buy them drinks.

He rested his left hand on top of one of the swing-doors and pushed it. He walked into the room and heard a stunned hush suddenly envelop the entire area. Even the man at the piano stopped playing half-way through a tune.

Iron Eyes walked slowly across the room towards the bar from where hundreds of bottles and glasses lured him on.

Iron Eyes knew that every one of the people inside the Wayward Gun were watching him.

But he did not care one bit. All he wanted to do was drink his fill of whiskey.

He ran the fingers of both hands through his limp, long, black hair and then stopped when he reached the bar. He rested one boot on the brass rail next to a spittoon and stared at the solitary bartender.

The man reluctantly approached the bounty hunter.

'A bottle of whiskey,' Iron Eyes whispered.

'We don't serve redskins in here. Get going,' the bartender said bluntly.

Iron Eyes lowered his head until his chin touched his bloodstained shirt collar. He took a deep breath, then, faster than the blink of an eye, grabbed the man's head with both hands and dragged him up over the bar counter.

Iron Eyes was furious. 'I ain't an Indian, you dumb bastard. Now get me a bottle of whiskey or I'll surely kill you.'

The startled man had never been so frightened before. He had looked into the eyes of the most dangerous bounty hunter in the West and survived.

He knew that Iron Eyes was not bluffing.

'OK, mister,' the bartender stuttered. 'Its ya hair. I ain't never seen a white man with such long black hair before. I'm sorry. Let me go and I'll get you your whiskey.'

Iron Eyes released his grip. The man felt his shoes hitting the floor again.

'Any particular brand of whiskey?'

'Good whiskey!' Iron Eyes slammed down a few coins and the bartender cautiously picked them up.

The bounty hunter used the reflection in the long mirror behind the bar to study the faces of the saloon's bemused patrons. Every one of them was staring at him with wide-eyed respect and terror.

Then Iron Eyes caught sight of his own image in the mirror as the bottle of whiskey was placed before him. It had been a long time since he had seen his own reflection and he was not pleased at the sight.

'Will this do, mister?' the bartender sheepishly asked.

Iron Eyes nodded. 'Yep. That'll do.'

The bartender began to wipe the wet counter with a cloth that had been draped over his shoulder. He kept looking at his tall customer. He had never seen a living man with such horrific injuries before. In fact, he had never seen a corpse with such injuries either.

'Are you OK, mister?' he eventually managed to ask.

Iron Eyes pulled the cork from the

bottle-neck with his teeth and spat it into the spittoon at his feet. He lifted the bottle to his lips and took a long hard swallow.

It was good liquor.

'Do I look OK?' Iron Eyes asked when he once again caught sight of his own image in the mirror.

'No, sir. You don't.'

'I've had me a real bad day.' The bounty hunter shrugged as he poured more of the fiery liquid into his mouth.

'You had an accident?' the bartender asked as he moved closer with his cloth.

'An accident?' Iron Eyes almost smiled. 'I reckon that's a darn good way of putting it, *amigo*. I've had me a day full of accidents. Real bad ones.'

The bartender moved closer. 'Do you need to see a doctor? We got one down the street. Reasonable rates.'

Iron Eyes swallowed more of the whiskey and then looked at the amber liquid in the clear bottle. He had consumed a third of the contents and knew that he could finish it off without its having any effect on him. For he had never once been able to get drunk and he had spent years trying real hard.

'You got any rooms for rent here?' Iron Eyes asked.

'We got one free room upstairs at the back of the building,' the bartender answered. 'Big Jack Brady has taken up the rest of them for his boys.'

'Big Jack Brady?' Iron Eyes repeated the name. He knew of the outlaw from his Wanted posters. He was worth $1,000 dead or alive.

The man behind the bar noticed the reaction in the bounty hunter's scarred face.

'You know him?'

'Only by reputation.' Iron Eyes took another sip of the whiskey and stared more closely at the saloon's layout. 'So Big Jack and his boys have rooms here, huh?'

'Yep. And a new one turned up today,' the bartender eagerly informed him.

'Harve Calhoon?' the bounty hunter

glanced at the man, who nodded.

'Yep. That was his name OK.'

Iron Eyes rubbed his chin. 'Don't the law mind so many outlaws hanging around Calico?'

'There ain't no law in the badlands, mister.' The bartender laughed. 'You sure got a keen sense of humour.'

'Yep. I sure have.' Iron Eyes nodded as the words sank into his tired brain. So this was the badlands. He had heard rumours of this place but until now had thought that they were just that. Mere rumours.

No wonder he had not seen a sheriff's office.

That would be the last thing the inhabitants of Calico would either need or want.

Iron Eyes rested the bottle on the counter and studied his appearance in the mirror again. What was left of his clothing barely covered his lean body. Everything he wore was either covered in blood or full of bullet holes. Or both.

'You got a store in this damn town

that sells trail clothes, *amigo?*' he asked.

'Yep. Won't be open until the morning, though,' the bartender replied. 'I can get you anything you want.'

'That's soon enough for me.' Iron Eyes pulled out a golden eagle from the bag in his pocket, rested it on the bar counter in front of the bartender, then stared at him. 'You go to that store in the morning and buy me some trail gear.'

'Same as you got on?'

'Yep. Shirt, pants and trail coat.' Iron Eyes nodded.

The bartender accepted the coin and tucked it into his vest pocket.

'Do you still want the room?'

Iron Eyes nodded.

The man plucked a key off the shelf behind him and handed it to the bounty hunter.

'Room twelve.'

Iron Eyes reached across the counter, pulled a cigar from the man's shirt pocket and placed it between his teeth.

The bartender struck a match and lit

the end of the cigar for Iron Eyes.

'Send another bottle up with a box of cigars,' Iron Eyes said as his lungs filled with the acrid smoke.

'What about the doctor?'

'The whiskey and cigars will do for now, *amigo*.'

The bartender nodded as his eyes watched the bounty hunter strolling across the quiet room towards the staircase with the bottle in his hand.

Slowly Iron Eyes climbed the staircase.

17

The bridge was big. Far bigger than he had ever imagined it would or could be. So big that Harve Calhoon had seen it when he and the rest of Big Jack Brady's team of hand-picked outlaws were more than a mile away from Honcho Wells.

Even the moonlight could not lessen its sheer awesome splendour.

Spanning the entire valley, Calhoon had quickly calculated that it had to be nearly 300 yards across and at least fifty foot high at the centre. The outlaw had seen bridges before but never one like this.

It was made up of thousands of large wooden trestles, bolted together and supporting the single-span tracks at its top, spanning the width of the valley.

Harve Calhoon started to get worried.

His mind tried to work out how much dynamite it would take to bring down such a magnificent structure. This was way beyond anything he had experience of. In the past, Calhoon had used explosives to blast a dozen or more bank vaults open with remarkable success but he had never once thought of demolishing a bridge.

Where did you start with something like this?

He focused on the trestles at the very base of the bridge. Was it possible to blow them apart and bring the rest down like a house of cards?

Calhoon had no idea how the bridge was constructed. He knew that he would have to get up close to see if he could find a weak point.

His mind wrestled with the problem as they continued to advance towards the bridge.

The river flowed swiftly between the wooden trestles at the base of the bridge. The high moon above made it appear that a thousand fireflies were dancing on the wide river.

The dozen horsemen and heavily laden wagon rode down on to the level ground next to the fast-flowing water.

Calhoon was riding next to the wide-shouldered giant Big Jack and could hear the man getting more and more excited the closer the long line of horses got to it.

'Looks mighty fine, huh?' Brady asked.

Calhoon grunted. 'Yep. Mighty fine, Big Jack.'

Every few paces of their horses, Calhoon glanced over his shoulder and watched as Black Roy Hart steered the wagon's four-horse team along the rugged route towards the place known as Honcho Wells.

He had inspected the explosives before they had ridden out of Calico a few hours earlier. There were thousands of sticks of top-grade nine-inch dynamite and boxes full of fuses on the flat bed of the wagon.

Calhoon began to think that he might

require every one of them to bring down a bridge so well constructed as the one before them.

The outlaw watched as Brady's huge right hand plucked a pocket-watch out of his coat and opened its golden cover.

'What's the time, Big Jack?' he asked.

'Four fifteen, Harve.' Brady smiled, patting him on the back for the umpteenth time. 'I can tell ya eager to start work on that bridge. Don't you fret none. We'll be there in less than half an hour.'

Calhoon cleared his dry throat.

'I can hardly wait.'

'We have between seven to eight hours for you to bring down that bridge and get all the boys in place ready to strike in the confusion,' Brady announced.

'What if the train is early, Big Jack?' Calhoon posed the question that most of the other men had thought of but none been brave enough to ask.

For the first time since he had met Brady, he saw the venom for which the big man was famed. The eyes widened and looked across the distance between the two lead horses. There was a madness in them.

'Ya better pray that the train is on schedule and you've blown the bridge apart before it reaches Honcho Wells, Harve,' Brady warned. ''Coz if it is early and ya ain't done your job, I'll surely kill ya.'

Harve Calhoon felt his throat tighten. He looked away from the angry face and stared again at the bridge. The closer they got to it, the bigger it looked.

'Understood, Big Jack,' Calhoon said as every bone in his body began to wish that he had stayed with the rest of his gang and headed on to Waco instead of riding to Calico.

It had been the promise of a big pay-day that had tempted him away from the rest of the Calhoon gang in the first place.

Now he was beginning to realize that one way or another, he might not live to collect.

18

Dynamite-man Harve Calhoon had taken the biggest gamble of his entire life. He had studied the high bridge from the banks of the river which flowed beneath it and decided that he did not have to bring the entire structure down to achieve what Big Jack Brady wanted.

The locomotive would have to stop even if only ten or twenty feet of the bridge was missing. If it didn't, then there would be one almighty mess in the valley.

It was more guesswork than anything, but he knew the damage the explosives could do if carefully placed in large enough quantities. Even though he had never had to demolish anything like the bridge before, he knew that it ought to fall once the dynamite bundles started to blow.

That was the theory.

Would the reality prove him correct?

Calhoon had strapped ten bundles of dynamite sticks to upright wooden trestles at the base of the bridge exactly at the point directly below where the bridge left the solid ground of the western side of the hilltop high above. His reckoning was simple, if he blew the lowest trestles away, the sheer weight of everything above ought to be too great for it to do anything but collapse.

Calhoon knew that it sounded logical, but he had to make sure by giving himself a second string to his destructive bow.

The outlaw filled a sack with bundles of dynamite sticks and some more fuses. He climbed up the trestles until he was standing on the railtracks high above the valley. The light of the moon gleamed off the steel tracks as they rested on the sleepers along the bridge. Calhoon squinted at them stretching off into infinity.

Calhoon knew that they might hold together even if he were to destroy everything beneath them. There was only one way to ensure that did not happen.

Carefully walking across the precarious wooden joists and trying not to look down, his skilled hands tied four bundles of dynamite sticks to the metal tracks roughly twenty feet from the start of the bridge. After inserting the fuse caps into the centre dynamite stick in the bundles he moved to the edge of the bridge and dropped the long fuse coil down to where the rest of the outlaws were watching his every move.

Harve Calhoon rubbed the sweat off his face and started to climb back down. He had ensured that the top and bottom of the first section of bridge would be blown apart; he just prayed that everything in between would follow suit.

Big Jack Brady watched Calhoon descending towards him and then turned to allow the light of the moon to illuminate the face of his pocket-watch.

It was nearly dawn.

He looked at the rest of his men.

'I want you all up there waiting on either side of the tracks for when that train gets here,' Brady said. 'Black Roy stays down here with me, Harve and the wagon. After all, there ain't no way we can move boxes of gold coin out of here without a wagon.'

'How many boxes of gold coin do you figure there'll be, Big Jack?' one of the outlaws asked as he gathered up his reins.

Brady smiled. 'Might be hundreds, boy.'

The gunhands nodded, mounted their horses and rode up the steep incline. They knew that they would have to wait hours for the train to arrive at Honcho Wells, but they were used to waiting.

Waiting and then killing.

It was what they did best.

That was why they had been chosen

by Brady from all the other outlaws who roamed the badlands. The big man knew whom he could rely upon to turn his ambitions into reality.

Big Jack Brady said nothing when Calhoon got to the base of the bridge. His hooded eyes watched, though, as the man wove the various long fuses together until he had just one in his gloved hands.

'You gotta match I can borrow, Big Jack?' Calhoon called out to Brady.

The big man reached into his vest pocket, hauled out a box of matches and tossed them across to the outlaw. Harve Calhoon smiled as he caught the box in his left hand.

'I thought that maybe you'd want to light this yourself, Big Jack.' Calhoon grinned.

Brady waved a huge hand at Black Roy Hart. 'Get the wagon away from here, Black Roy. I don't wanna have it crushed by all the timber that'll be fallin'.'

Hart scurried up the side of the

wagon, grabbed hold of the reins and hauled them to his left. He released the brakepole and then got the team of horses moving.

'How far shall I take it, Big Jack?' Black Roy shouted down from the driver's seat.

Brady pointed down the riverbank. 'About a quarter mile should be OK. Now git going.'

Calhoon suddenly noticed that the sky above them was changing colour. The sunlight traced across the cloudless sky faster than the blink of an eye. He glanced across to the mouth of the valley and noticed that the sun was starting to rise.

'You sure you don't wanna light the fuse?' he asked the big man again.

Brady did not reply. He was walking away from the bridge with his horse on a short rein. There was an urgency in his step that told Harve Calhoon a lot about the man who liked to pretend that nothing frightened him.

But Calhoon could sense the truth,

he was afraid of the dynamite and it showed.

Harve Calhoon opened the box and pulled out a match. He looked up the embankment at the rest of the gang, who had just reached the flat ground near the steel rails.

'You better take cover up there, boys!' Calhoon yelled at the top of his lungs. 'There's gonna be an awful big bang in a couple of minutes.'

The outlaws pulled their reins hard and turned their dust-caked mounts. Then they galloped away.

Harve Calhoon turned away from the rising dust that drifted into the morning air. He glanced back at Brady, running now as he desperately sought cover.

The outlaw struck the match along the side of the box and cupped the flame carefully to the end of the fuses. For a few seconds nothing happened. Then they burst into spitting fiery action.

The outlaw who was known as the dynamite man carefully lowered the fuse to the ground and watched it for a moment. When satisfied that it would not go out, he strode to his waiting horse, stepped into the stirrup and hurriedly mounted. He swung the horse around and jabbed his spurs.

The horse sprang into action. Calhoon rode after the fleeing Brady and the wagon.

The ground was hard along the riverbank. The outlaw had no idea at what speed the fuses would burn to reach the explosives but he had no intention of waiting to find out. He hoped that they had roughly a couple of minutes before the first explosion, but even that was a guess.

As he urged the mount on he realized how much easier it was to blow open bank vaults.

When Calhoon reached the puffing Brady, he stopped his mount and looked down at him. He pointed at the wagon, which was another few hundred yards further along the riverbank.

'I reckon that Black Roy's about the

right distance away from the bridge, Big Jack.' Calhoon smiled, then spurred his horse and galloped to where the wagon was waiting. Brady grabbed hold of his saddle horn, hauled his immense bulk on to his saddle and followed.

Just as the large rider reached the wagon and the two men who were taking cover behind it, the first of the dynamite bundles strapped to the bridge trestles exploded. Within seconds, the rest of them blasted.

None of the three outlaws had ever heard anything like it.

It hurt.

The massive bulk of Brady scrambled off his saddle to the ground and stared in disbelief at the sight of scores of well-placed explosives igniting into deafening action.

The dynamite bundles exploded one after another at intervals of a few seconds. The explosions went up the trestles at ten-foot intervals until the burning fuses reached the rails at the very top.

Then it was like a volcano erupting.

Fire and smoke shot hundreds of feet into the morning air as plumes of dust were blasted off the dry valley wall. Even more black smoke and debris spewed out in every direction as the shock waves sent clouds of choking dust over the entire area.

Suddenly Brady dived beside Calhoon and Black Roy. The pair of outlaws had no chance to ask why. Thousands of fragments of wood showered over them and the wagon.

Their startled horses reared up and vainly kicked out at the very air itself.

The smouldering downpour seemed to last for ever as the stench of burning wood filled their nostrils. Blinding dust swept over the trio as they tried to breathe and the wagon above them shook violently. At last the deafening explosions gradually stopped as the smoke and dust drifted across the river, leaving the three men lying beside the wagon.

Harve Calhoon was first to his feet.

His keen eyes squinted into the sun as he looked at the bridge. It seemed an eternity before the billowing smoke thinned out enough for him to see his handiwork.

As Brady staggered to his feet and leant on the side of the wagon next to him, Calhoon felt a sudden relief overwhelming him.

He had done it.

He had completely demolished a quarter of the massive bridge with only half the dynamite in the wagon.

'You done it, Harve!' Big Jack yelled happily. 'You blew the hell out of the damn thing.'

'I sure did.' Calhoon leaned on the tailgate of the wagon and looked at the unused sticks of dynamite and boxes of fuses still under the tarp.

'The train will have to stop now!'

Black Roy was hitting the side of his head frantically.

'I can't hear nothin',' he wailed.

Harve Calhoon looked into the wagon at the surplus dynamite.

'Reckon you'll want to dump this here to make room for the gold, Big Jack?'

Brady shook his head. 'Nope. I ain't throwing that dynamite away, boy. It'll come in useful on our next job. Besides, it cost a lot of money.'

Black Roy got to his feet and kept rubbing his ears in a vain attempt to stop the ringing inside his head.

'I'm deaf,' he shouted.

'Let's hope it's permanent,' Brady chuckled.

'Yeah.' Calhoon rubbed the dust off his face. He had a feeling in his craw that it might not be easy to ride away from Big Jack Brady.

In fact, it might be impossible.

19

The explosions at Honcho Wells rattled the windows of every building in Calico, but few were awake at dawn to notice. Only one man noticed. He stared at the window in his small room above the Wayward Gun saloon.

Iron Eyes had not slept during the night. He had just been smoking one cigar after another and sipping his whiskey from the neck of his second bottle.

Even though the distant explosion had shaken the entire badlands, Iron Eyes seemed unconcerned. He did not bother to get up from the bed that he was lying upon, with his primed Navy Colts to each side of his lean, scarred body.

When the panes stopped rattling in the window-frames he looked back at the hotel door. It was bolted against any unexpected intruder wishing to claim the life of the infamous bounty hunter.

Iron Eyes wondered whether any of the hard-drinking men who had been in the saloon when he arrived might have recognized him. If they had it was only a matter of time before they came looking for blood.

His blood.

His only consolation was that covered in sandfilled wounds he might not have looked his awesome worst. Maybe the sight had made the witnesses to his arrival in the saloon think that it was impossible they had been actually looking at Iron Eyes himself. For the myth of his apparent invincibility was known far and wide.

Either way, he could not give a damn.

If they came looking for him, he would kill them. It was as simple as that.

Iron Eyes thought about the explosions again. He knew that Harve Calhoon must have had something to do with them, because it mentioned that he was an expert with dynamite on the crumpled Wanted poster.

He sucked on the wet end of the cigar, then nodded to himself as his eyes continued to stare at the door of the room.

At last he knew why the outlaw had left the rest of his gang and ridden here. It had something to do with Big Jack Brady's needing a man of Calhoon's talents.

Iron Eyes wondered what he had blown up.

He knew that it must have been big for it to be felt here in this remote town. But his curiosity was not like other men's. He could wait to find out.

Suddenly a knock came at the door.

The long thin fingers of the bounty hunter clawed the Navy Colts into his hands and stroked the gun metal fondly. His head was propped up by three pillows so that he could see the door at all times.

'Who is it?'

'The barkeep, sir,' came the recognizable voice from the other side of the wooden door.

'What you want?'

'I brung you the clothes that you wanted and another bottle of whiskey,' the bartender replied.

Iron Eyes' thumbs hauled the hammers of his twin pistols back until they locked fully.

'I thought you said that the clothes store didn't open until about ten?'

'It don't. But the owner came in for a few drinks and I got him to open up early.' The man's voice sounded nervous.

Iron Eyes raised himself up until he was sitting. He swung his long naked legs off the soft mattress and placed his feet on the floorboards.

He stood and walked silently to the door with both his Navy Colts at hip level. Iron Eyes used the barrel of the gun in his left hand to slide the bolt across before stepping backwards two paces.

'Come in real slow, *amigo*.' His voice had a warning in it.

A warning that the bartender heeded.

The cold grey eyes watched the door handle turn and the door open towards him. His fingers were resting on the triggers of the guns waiting to see if this was yet another trick.

There had been so many in his long life.

The bartender entered with the clothes over one arm and a bottle of whiskey under the other. He tried not to look at the tall naked figure as he made his way to the bed and placed everything on top of the crumpled sheet.

Iron Eyes kept the guns trained on the man.

'You did OK,' the bounty hunter said, looking at the new clothes.

The bartender tried to avert his eyes from the scarred body before him. He had never seen such injuries on anyone before and it upset him.

'Are them knife wounds, sir?'

Iron Eyes nodded. 'Yep. I had me a disagreement with some Apaches.'

The bartender cleared his throat and offered the tall man his change from the golden eagle coin.

Iron Eyes shook his head. He placed one of his guns on the bed and lifted up the pants.

'Keep the change,' he said.

The bartender moved to the door and then looked back at the figure. It seemed impossible that anyone could have such gruesome injuries and still be capable of functioning.

'I got me a feeling that you ain't an outlaw like the rest of the folks in Calico.'

Iron Eyes glanced at him. 'Let's keep that a secret, *amigo*. I've had me too many accidents in the past twenty-four hours.'

'I ain't no gossip, sir.'

The man closed the door and made his way along the corridor to the stairs. As he walked down the carpeted steps he heard the bolt being pushed back into place in room twelve.

20

Captain Wallis's face went ashen as the deafening echoes eventually faded from Devil's Pass. The seasoned officer had stopped his men when the first crescendo of explosions began echoing off the canyon walls.

He sat silently as Sergeant Hanks moved his sweating mount next to the tall charger.

'Reckon that's got anything to do with ya orders, sir?' Hanks asked as he steadied his nervous horse and thought about the secret papers he had been allowed to read hours earlier. Papers that ordered them to investigate the goings-on within the Indian Territory.

Wallis looked across at the brooding trooper. Hanks's face reflected the same concern that was etched on the eighty other cavalrymen.

'That sounded as if it came from the

territories to me,' the captain said. 'What do you think, Hanks?'

Hanks nodded. 'Reckon ya right.'

The captain's attention was drawn to Billy Bodine, who had reached their ranks hours earlier with his tall story about Apaches waiting to ambush them. Wallis had thought then that the young trooper had simply had too much sun the previous day and then allowed his vivid imagination to run unchecked. Now with the violent explosions still ringing in his ears, he was not so sure that Bodine was imagining things.

He was simply misinterpreting them.

'Come here, Billy,' Wallis called out.

Bodine spurred his quarter horse to the side of the captain and Hanks.

'Yes, Captain?'

'How far are we from the narrow side-canyon that you said had two sets of horse tracks?' Wallis asked.

Bodine smiled. At last the man was starting to believe him.

'It's hard to tell in daylight, but as

best as I can figure, it can only be another mile or so.'

Hanks looked at the thoughtful officer.

'You don't believe the rubbish that young Billy here was spouting earlier, do ya?'

Wallis looked at the shimmering trail ahead of them. They were now right in the heart of Devil's Pass.

'I never doubted that Billy saw tracks, but I got me an idea that he just didn't know what they meant.'

Billy leaned forward in his saddle.

'What is our mission, Captain?'

Wallis glanced at Hanks and then returned his attention to the youthful trooper.

'I'll tell you, Billy,' he began. 'There are rumours that the Indian Territory has been taken over by outlaws. That's why we've been getting news at Fort Dixon of various bands of Indians roaming around outside their designated land.'

Hanks looked at the younger rider.

'Our mission is to go into the Indian land and see for ourselves what's happening.'

Bodine swallowed hard.

'Ride into Indian land?'

Wallis smiled. 'That's about it. Lead the way to that canyon you found the tracks in, Billy.'

Reluctantly, the trooper spurred his chestnut mount on. The captain waved his arm and the platoon started on after the quarter horse.

Hanks scratched his side-whiskers.

'Do ya think this is a real smart thing for us to be doing, sir?'

'Orders don't have to be smart,' the captain answered, 'they have to be obeyed.'

Hanks sighed heavily. 'Which do ya reckon is worse, sir, outlaws or Indians?'

Wallis looked at Hanks.

'I was just wondering that myself.'

'That don't settle me down none.'

Wallis allowed his charger to gather pace behind Bodine.

'But ask yourself something, old friend. Do you think that Indians would or could have created that explosion we heard a while back?'

Sergeant Hanks allowed his horse to keep pace with his superior's mount and thought about the question.

Hanks had no answer for it.

★ ★ ★

Blood ran down the steep incline towards the river which continued to flow swiftly beneath what was left of the bridge. The bullet-ridden bodies were littered over the high embankment and railtracks next to the carriages behind the huge locomotive, which had come to an abrupt halt just before the destroyed bridge. Those who had managed to survive the bullets had been hacked to death.

The train had arrived at Honcho Wells on schedule. It had taken less than ten minutes for Big Jack Brady's hired killers to storm its meagre defences and kill every man who tried vainly to protect its valuable cargo.

They were good at their job.

Their lethal gun-skills had been honed by anger and impatience while waiting in the blazing sun for hours. Yet the true fury was born long before in minds that saw nothing wrong with slaughtering anyone who defied them.

It was a madness that made them valuable to people like Big Jack Brady.

Brady had watched from the safe distance he had put between himself and the men who he knew would kill for the price of a bottle of whiskey, let alone an equal share of the profits with which he had tempted them.

His massive bulk shook with excitement as he listened to every unheeded scream.

The slaughter had gone on for far longer than it would have taken just to kill those who were hired to protect the army gold. The big man knew that once his hand-picked team of murderers tasted the blood of their victims, they would not stop until every single living creature on the train had also been brutally killed.

It was a knowledge that he had kept from the dynamite man.

Harve Calhoon had said nothing as he watched and listened in horror from beside the wagon with Black Roy Hart and the excited Brady as the carnage was carried out above them.

The outlaw felt his stomach turn over when his ears picked up the unmistakable sound of women and children screaming in the carriages of the helpless train.

The gunshots ended all the pitiful pleas for mercy that drifted on the warm air towards them.

Every one of his misgivings about working for Brady had been realized. The outlaw felt sick, yet he knew that it would be suicidal to voice his objections. He had already done his job and was now expendable.

'They done it, Harve,' Brady said, gleefully clapping his hands together. 'I told ya that them boys are the best there is in all of the badlands. They know how to kill.'

Calhoon had robbed many banks in his time but he had never been involved in anything like this.

It was like a nightmare.

'I told ya that my boys are the best,' Brady repeatedly boomed as his huge hand pointed at his men who were now throwing large metal strongboxes down into the valley.

Calhoon stood and rubbed the sweat off his mouth. His eyes saw Black Roy's face. It bore the same fevered expression as was etched on that of Big Jack.

The grin seemed to go from ear to ear.

'We had better take the wagon to the bottom of the slope, boys, and collect all them strongboxes,' Big Jack Brady gushed eagerly. 'I want that gold on the flatbed.'

Calhoon said nothing as he gathered up his reins and watched the huge man climbing up on to the driver's seat of the wagon, next to Black Roy.

The smaller man lashed the long reins down hard on the backs of the four-horse team. He guided the wagon along the riverbank to where the strongboxes were piling up.

Harve Calhoon mounted and sat in his saddle, watching in disbelief. He wanted to ride away from this blood-bath but knew he would not reach safety before a bullet found his back.

He teased his horse after the wagon and wondered if he would survive once Brady had realized that he no longer needed him.

21

Iron Eyes had not lost any of his instincts over the years since he had stopped hunting animals and had transferred his lethal skills to tracking down men for the price upon their heads. He could wait. For as long as it took, he would wait.

For hunters had patience.

That was what made him the most dangerous of all the bounty hunters who roamed the West looking for the elusive outlaws who had managed to make themselves more valuable dead than alive.

Harve Calhoon had no idea what fate the rest of his gang had met at the hands of Iron Eyes at Waco. He would return to Calico unaware that the skeletal hands of the famed Iron Eyes would be aiming his deadly Navy Colts at him. There was still one creased and worn Wanted poster remaining in the deep bullet-filled pocket of the brand-new trail coat that had yet to be claimed.

Iron Eyes had not slept since realizing that he still had one of the notorious Calhoon gang left to kill.

The bounty hunter had not wasted a single minute of the long hot day. He knew that wherever Harve Calhoon and the rest of Brady's gang had disappeared to, they would have eventually to return to Calico.

He had been standing on the boardwalk outside the Wayward Gun watching the sun slowly setting for more than two hours. If anyone in the busy outlaw town had recognized his brutalized features, they had kept it to themselves.

Iron Eyes stood like a statue in his new clothes, watching.

Watching and waiting.

The cold, calculating eyes blinked only occasionally as he stared out at the trail along which he knew his prey would come. He did not have to do anything except bide his time until the outlaw came into his web.

The sky above Calico went red as the sun fell beneath the horizon. Darkness was slow to envelop the township as Iron Eyes watched men moving along the streets, lighting the street-lanterns.

The boards behind the tall waiting figure creaked but Iron Eyes did not turn to look to see who it was. He knew it was the bartender returning to the Wayward Gun to start work again.

'You still here?' the man asked.

Iron Eyes grunted. He struck a match with his thumbnail, lifted it to the end of the long thin cigar and inhaled.

The bartender moved closer and stared at the pair of gun grips that poked out from just above the belt buckle. He had never before seen anyone use his pants rather than a gunbelt and holster to support his weapons.

'How come you don't use holsters,

sir?' the man asked respectfully.

Iron Eyes glanced down at the bartender. He could not understand why he seemed continually to hang around him.

'I don't need holsters,' came the simple reply.

The bartender nodded. 'Have you eaten?'

'Nope. Not yet.'

The man looked at the trail road that led off to the distant Honcho Wells and then back at the bounty hunter.

'Who are you waiting for?'

'Harve Calhoon.' Iron Eyes said the name as smoke drifted through his teeth.

'But he's in with Big Jack Brady and his men,' the bartender warned him. 'They'll not give up one of their own without a fight.'

'If they want to fight, I'll oblige them.'

'Who are you?' the bartender asked quietly.

'Reckon it's best that you don't know

that, mister.' The reply came quietly from Iron Eyes' lips.

The bartender nodded and began to move away towards the saloon's swing-doors. Then he paused and stared at the awesome figure who continued to focus on the trail as the evening grew darker and darker.

'You gonna kill this Calhoon critter?'

Iron Eyes flicked the ash from his cigar.

'Yep.'

★　★　★

The dozen riders surrounded the wagon when it rolled into the quiet streets of Calico. Harve Calhoon knew that he had to say nothing and simply go along with the brutal Brady if he were to have even half a chance of getting out of the badlands alive.

The street-lanterns flickered as Black Roy Hart hauled the wagon reins to his chest and then pushed the brake pole on with his foot.

The men who stopped their horses all around the wagon wanted their share of the army gold payroll and it showed in their gruesome expressions.

Big Jack Brady carefully manoeuvred his 300-pound bulk down from the driver's seat of the wagon to the ground. He hauled the tarp back and stared at the eight strongboxes lying next to the remainder of the dynamite and fuses.

Even in the light which escaped from the large store windows on to the street, Calhoon could clearly see Brady drooling as if he were looking at one of the countless meals he must have consumed in his life.

Brady studied the padlock of the closest of the large metal boxes and then hauled one of his pistols from its holster. He aimed at the padlock and squeezed the trigger.

The bullet shattered the lock into a thousand fragments.

Brady rammed his gun back into its holster. He pulled up the steel flap of the box and lifted the heavy lid.

He had never seen so many freshly minted golden eagles in all his days. Drool dripped from his open mouth.

'Look at it, boys. We struck paydirt and no mistake.'

Harve Calhoon dismounted and led his horse to the closest hitching rail and wrapped the reins around it. He kept trying to tell himself that he was an outlaw and this was what his kind did, but it did not work.

However bad he thought he was, he was a saint in comparison to these men.

'We sharing it out now?' one of the riders asked in a voice that caused all the other horsemen to nod in agreement.

Brady lowered the lid of the strongbox and turned to face the riders who encircled him.

His eyes sought out the one who had asked the question.

'Nope. We ain't.'

The riders began to mutter amongst themselves as they eased their horses closer to the huge man.

'We want our share now, Brady,' shouted another of them.

Harve Calhoon stood beside his mount. He saw the figures coming out of the various buildings into the wide street. It was as if every outlaw in Calico could smell the gold within the boundaries of their town.

Big Jack waved a finger at the horsemen.

'We can't stay in Calico, boys. We have to hightail it out of here if we are gonna share out this loot.'

They did not seem to like the idea.

'We want our share now, Big Jack.'

Brady felt the hair on the back of his fat neck tingle but he defied his own fears and stayed firmly planted to the spot.

'The army will come swarming in here as soon as they discover the train, boys. We have to get out of the badlands and head south. Then we can split the money equally.'

The words did not seem to wash with

the mounted gunmen.

'Some folks might say that old Big Jack is trying to run a scam on us, boys,' growled one of the riders. His fellow outlaws all grunted in agreement.

Big Jack Brady's eyes searched the faces of the onlookers as his mind wondered where his personal bodyguards were. He had left them in Calico when he had headed to Honcho Wells with this bunch of killers. Now he needed them to back him up.

'This is a mistake, boys.' He tried to convince them. 'Even Calico ain't no protection should the army come looking for its money. Can't you understand that?'

Suddenly the crowd made a unified gasp.

Brady and the riders all turned to face the crowd which had gathered outside the Wayward Gun saloon. Even in the lanternlight, it was clear that a tall figure was moving down from the boardwalk.

Each of the outlaws around Brady turned his horse to square up to the tall, emaciated figure before them.

'You're just like a bunch of hyenas fighting over a rotting carcass,' Iron Eyes said loud enough for Brady and all of his followers to hear.

'Who the hell is that?' Brady asked. He stepped away from the wagon and rested his hands on the grips of his guns.

A mumble went through his hired riders until one name became clearly audible.

'Iron Eyes!' they all seemed to say at once.

'Iron Eyes?' Even Big Jack Brady had heard of the infamous bounty hunter.

The man who looked more dead than alive stepped out into the light that bathed the street and allowed them to study his hideous features in more detail. He rested his bony hands on his hips and lowered his head.

Iron Eyes stared through his long, limp hair at the men who faced him. It was a look that many men had seen just before he had killed them.

'That's right. I'm Iron Eyes.'

Brady defiantly took another step forward.

'The stinking bounty hunter?'

A wry smile etched Iron Eyes' scarred face,

'Yep,' he agreed.

Brady waved his left arm at his riders. 'Kill him!'

The order was loud enough to echo off the wooden walls of every building in Calico. The men frantically reached for their guns.

Before the first outlaw's finger had found its trigger, Iron Eyes had hauled both his Navy Colts from his belt and thrown himself sideways towards the line of horses tied up outside the saloon.

Bullets tore through the air towards the thin figure. Iron Eyes rolled over until he was on one knee. His deadly aim had not deserted him.

With every beat of his heart, Iron

Eyes shot one outlaw after another off his horse as Black Roy jumped to the ground and Brady ducked behind the wagon.

A half-dozen bullets sprayed into the horse beside the kneeling bounty hunter. He heard a pitiful whinny and then had to dive backwards as the heavy creature landed heavily beside him.

Iron Eyes narrowed his icy stare and watched silently as the crowd disappeared as quickly as it had appeared. Bullets were cutting across the warm night air in both directions as Iron Eyes crawled beneath the nearest boardwalk and hastily reloaded his guns.

He snapped shut the smoking chambers of both Navy Colts, and scurried beneath the building until he reached its corner. Iron Eyes hauled himself back to his feet and leaned against the wall.

Shadows were now his only ally.

Those of the riders who were left

were still shooting in the direction of the fallen horse. He counted five men left in their saddles and Brady and Black Roy Hart hiding behind the wagon.

His mind told him that he had had twelve bullets and there were only seven of them left.

Without a second thought for his own safety, the bounty hunter stepped away from the building and fired again as he advanced towards them.

Before any of Brady's hired killers knew what was happening, the deadly accuracy of Iron Eyes' Navy Colts had brought them off their saddles. Then he turned his attention to the men behind the wagon.

Iron Eyes knelt and stared under the belly of the heavily laden vehicle. He could see movement. He pulled back the hammer of the pistol in his left hand and fired.

The sound of a man shouting angrily filled his ears. He rose back to his full height and fired again as he raced across the distance between them.

When he was within twenty feet of the back of the wagon, he saw a figure rising and aiming his guns at him.

Both men fired at exactly the same time.

Black Roy's head shattered as the bullet hit it dead centre but as the man fell forward and hit the ground, his dead fingers caused the hair-triggers to fire again.

Iron Eyes felt himself turning on his heels as the impact in his left shoulder knocked him off balance. He staggered and fell towards the wagon.

The metal wheel-rim caught the side of the bounty hunter's temple just before he crashed to the ground. He tried to move but he was too dazed.

Suddenly the huge figure of Big Jack Brady loomed over Iron Eyes. The stunned bounty hunter tried to raise his weapons but he could not.

He was helpless.

Then he saw the barrels of Brady's guns aimed at his face.

'You're gonna die, you evil bastard!' the man yelled down at him.

The sound of the gunfire was deafening.

Finale

As blood traced down the side of his head, Iron Eyes began to focus on the body beside him. It was Brady. A bullet hole in the middle of his forehead told the injured bounty hunter that the hefty outlaw was no longer a threat to anyone.

Then he felt two hands on his arms.

Iron Eyes was raised to his feet by Harve Calhoon and the bartender. Both men seemed to be checking the neat hole in his shoulder at the same time.

'The bullet went straight through,' the bartender said.

'It ain't even bleeding,' Calhoon added.

Iron Eyes rested his back against the wagon and managed to focus on the two men. He then saw the smoking pistol in Harve Calhoon's hand.

'Did you kill the fat man, mister?'

Calhoon nodded. 'Yep. I couldn't let him get away with killing you.'

'Why not?'

'That gang just slaughtered a whole bunch of innocent folks back at Honcho Wells,' Calhoon explained. 'Even women and kids.'

'Vermin,' the bounty hunter growled.

'They were lower than vermin, Iron Eyes.' Calhoon sighed.

Iron Eyes rubbed the blood off his face with his sleeve and studied the outlaw before him. The face was carved into his mind, he had seen it on the poster in his pocket.

'Harve Calhoon,' Iron Eyes said drily.

'That's my name. You know me?' Calhoon asked. He lifted the pair of Navy Colts off the sand and handed them to the injured bounty hunter.

For a moment Iron Eyes said nothing. He had trailed this man for weeks and yet for some reason which he could not fathom, the man had saved his life.

'I reckon I ought to thank you, mister.' Iron Eyes slid both his pistols into his belt and pulled himself away from the side of the wagon.

Suddenly the sound of an army bugle filled the streets of Calico. The three men watched as every outlaw in the town came running out of the saloons and gambling-halls and running to their mounts.

As the sound of the approaching platoon of cavalrymen grew louder, hundreds of men galloped out of the town.

Iron Eyes turned and looked at Harve Calhoon.

'Ride, Calhoon. The army will slap you in shackles if ya still here when they arrive.'

'Reckon ya right, Iron Eyes.'

The outlaw touched the brim of his Stetson and ran to his horse. He threw himself on to its saddle. The man thundered after the fleeing outlaws.

The bartender took hold of the bounty hunter's elbow and helped him to the empty boardwalk outside the Wayward Gun. Iron Eyes sat down on the steps and pulled out a cigar, which he placed between his teeth. He watched as the bartender seated himself next to him.

'I thought ya was gonna kill Harve Calhoon?'

Iron Eyes chewed on the cigar and stared at the bodies before them.

'There's enough bounty on the ground here for me, friend.'

'And ya might get a reward for recovering the army gold.' The bartender grinned.

'I hadn't thought of that.' Iron Eyes accepted a light for his cigar and inhaled the smoke deeply. 'What they call you?'

'John Smith.' The man smiled sheepishly.

Iron Eyes nodded. They could hear the troopers horses entering the outskirts of Calico.

'I believe ya, but a lot of folks wouldn't.'

'Are you about ready to see a doctor now?' the man asked.

Iron Eyes chewed on the cigar.

'I'm giving it serious consideration, Mr Smith.'

THE CHISELLER

Tex Larrigan

Soon the paddle steamer would be on its long journey down the Missouri River to St Louis. Now, all Saul Rhymer had to do was to play the last master stroke of the evening. He looked at the mounting pile of gold and dollar bills and again at the cards in his hand. Then, looking around the table, he produced the deed to the goldmine in Montana. 'Let's play poker!' But little did he know how that journey back to St Louis would change his life so drastically.

THE ARIZONA KID

Andrew McBride

When former hired gun Calvin Taylor took the job of sheriff of Oxford County, New Mexico, it was for one reason only — to catch, or kill, the notorious Arizona Kid, and pick up the fifteen hundred dollars reward the governor had secretly offered. Taylor found himself on the trail of the infamous gang known as the Regulators, hunting down a man who'd once been his friend. The pursuit became, in every sense, a journey of death.

BULLETS IN BUZZARDS CREEK

Bret Rey

The discovery of a dead saloon girl is only the beginning of Sheriff Jeff Gilpin's problems. Fortunately, his old friend 'Doc' Holliday arrives in Buzzards Creek just as Gilpin is faced by an outlaw gang. In a dramatic shoot-out the sheriff kills their leader and Holliday's reputation scares the hell out of the others. But it isn't long before the outlaws return, when they know Holliday is not around, and Gilpin is alone against six men . . .

THE YANKEE HANGMAN

Cole Rickard

Dan Tate was given a virtually impossible task: to save the murderer Jack Williams from the condemned cell. Williams, scum that he was, held a secret that was dear to the Confederate cause. But if saving Williams would test all Dan's ingenuity, then his further mission called for immense courage and daring. His life was truly on the line and if he didn't succeed, Horace Honeywell, the Yankee Hangman would have the last word!

MISSOURI PALACE

S. J. Rodgers

When ex-lawman Jim Williams accepts the post of security officer on the *Missouri Palace* riverboat, he finds himself embroiled in a power struggle between Captain J. D. Harris and Jake Farrell, the murderous boss of Willow Flats, who will stop at nothing to add the giant sidepaddler to his fleet. Williams knows that with no one to back him up in a straight fight with Farrell's hired killers, he must hit them first and hit them hard to get out alive.